china scoop

Also by Denis Miller

The Chinese Jade Affair
Diplomatic Traffic
A Spell in Normandy

china scoop

Denis Miller

AESOP Modern Fiction
Oxford

AESOP Modern Fiction
An imprint of AESOP Publications
Martin Noble Editorial / AESOP
28 Abberbury Road, Oxford OX4 4ES, UK
www.mne-aesop.com

First edition published by AESOP Publications
Copyright (c) 2012 Denis Miller

A catalogue record of this book is
available from the British Library.

First edition 2012

**FT
Pbk**

ISBN: 978-0-9569098-9-3

Printed and bound in Great Britain by
Lightning Source UK Ltd,
Chapter House, Pitfield, Kiln Farm,
Milton Keynes MK11 3LW

acknowledgement

For some scraps of Australian dialogue, I am indebted to a lexicon compiled by Afferbeck Lauder, Professor of Strine Studies, University of Sinny; this booklet (published by Ure Smith, Sydney, 1965) has long been considered useful if not obligatory reading for all stewnce, vistas and 'New Strines' – of which the writer is one.

DM

prologue

'**D**O YOU remember me?'

I put the question to a fit-looking but elderly man in a tracksuit bottom and white sweater edged with light-blue that suggested a Cambridge past. He had just joined me in a shedlike structure attached to a sports hall used by a local school in Gerrards Cross. The shed, more of a cubicle really, serves as an office.

The man I was addressing had come off the court after badminton coaching some youngsters. A noisy group of them scampered past the office door. The coach had a last word for one of the pack:

'Stephen, put your bloody racket straight in the press – now! You'll forget, and you know these things are fragile and warp easily ...'

He gave a friendly wave to the offender and then turned his attention to me. There was a blank look for an instant and then, with a slight shake of the head, a bemused smile deepened the lines on his face. He didn't recognise me.

True, I had put on a lot of weight since we last met, now wore glasses and my thinning hair was grey. But I certainly recognised *him,* this tall, athletically slim Chinese, with his easy Western bearing. He wore his age much better than me, and the impeccable silver hair that I remembered seemed not to have changed at all. I noticed the three-inch scar on his right cheek. And I knew how he had come by it.

'Well, sorry, but I can't place you at all ...' He flopped down at a small table. '... I mean, are you interested in badminton?'

'No, Mr Tan, not exactly—'

Suddenly his eyes shot up, and there was a broad smile.

7

'Nobody's called me *Tan* for a long time! When I moved to England twenty years ago, everybody for some reason started using the Mandarin version of my name, so I've been known here as Gerry *Chen* ever since!' He leaned forward and nudged the other chair in a polite gesture for me to sit as well.

The packet under my arm was vaguely bothering me. I put the roughly bound-up typescript down on the table, across which Chen was sitting. On the top sheet of the bundle was scribbled with a felt pen the name 'Denis Miller'.

'So ... if it's not badminton—'

'As a matter of fact – well, just in passing – my grandfather was an All-England champion back in the twenties.'

'*What?* Good heavens ... How splendid! What's the name – we'll have a look ...' Chen jumped up and grabbed a handbook from a shelf.

'Sautter,' I said. Chen flicked through the pages and then ran his finger down a list.

'Yes, indeed ... Here we are ... Guy Sautter ... and *three* times – and, I see, once as runner-up!' He beamed at me. 'You must play, too?'

'I don't,' I said, 'and actually I didn't come to talk about badminton.'

'All right.' Chen offered a smiling open-hands flutter of invitation. 'What can I do for you, Mr Sautter?' He sat down again.

'In fact, that's not my name. More precisely, he was my *step*-grandfather.'

'Ah ... sorry.' He glanced at the packet on the table. 'Perhaps I should have said "Mr Miller"?' His eyes turned to me again. There may have been, even then, a faint tightening in his face before I spoke again.

'You once bribed me not to publish an article ... And, of course, I actually saw you getting your scar,' I said, with as much deadpan as I could. We stared at one another for a moment.

'Good God ...!' There was a pause, but recognition had indeed come.

'Fenton!' he exclaimed, leaning back in his chair. With astonishing aplomb, he added: *'Bribed?* Come, come now ... But very clever of you to have tracked me down here. I do this coaching just once a week to keep me on my toes. I live locally, but am in London most of the time – boring consultancy work.'

'I know,' I said, 'I'm still a journalist.'

'Yes...' he said, leaning into the word. 'Well ... again ... what can I do for you?'

'You'll be aware that, as *agreed* ...' My face must have shown an involuntary grimace at the use of the word '... no article was published. But I've now written a book.' I flapped a hand at the typescript. 'Theoretically, fiction of course. It's rough and incomplete, but I thought that you should have the chance to fill in some detail for me. For a start, I'd like to know just how you've managed to keep out of jail and—'

A short laugh and a dismissive wave cut me off.

'I must ask ...' he said slowly. The light tapping of his fingers on the table kept pace for a second or two's reflection. '... How is Mrs ... Mrs Waley, or perhaps now your *wife*...?' The man's relaxed assurance was still the same as ever.

'She's fine. I'll leave the script with you. You can let me know – details are here.' It was curt and brief. I put a name card on the table. I was determined not to let this extraordinary man unnerve me again – as he had done years ago.

'The cottage address on the card will anyway no doubt ring bells for you ...' I got up, and Chen – sometime Tan – ushered me the few steps to the door. The opposite entrance-way to the gymnasium was still open. With night closing in, the interior was now half-darkened and eerily deserted.

'So, on reading though it, I'm sure you'll quickly see what parts need to be, let's say, developed ... or even changed.' I tried to make the tone one of certain authority, not to say of instruction.

'Doubt that I'll be of much use,' Gerry Chen said casually, with another smile, 'but I'll do what I can.' His comment came with the polite diffidence of someone with a sprained wrist agreeing to help move a wardrobe.

'You owe me this,' I said.

And in farewell, we even shook hands.

one

Rome, 1978

'Have a nice holiday, Signor Fenton – *grazie, grazie!*'

The old *portiera* thrust the keys of Fenton's apartment into her apron pocket, along with the 10,000 lira note. He was accustomed to doing it, but felt a twinge of anxiety at leaving the keys with the concierge, and this time, two weeks' absence would be longer than usual for him. She stood there wringing her arthritic hands, watching closely as Fenton humped his suitcase towards the waiting taxi. The leather-jacketed driver took one look at his charge, and leapt forward to help. He knew a good fare when he saw one.

Despite his long expatriate status, Larry Fenton still looked very 'English'. He stood just over six feet tall, slightly stooping, and was good-looking in a disinterested, non-aggressive way. The light linen washed-out beige suit he wore today had originally been well cut, but the trousers were now an inch too short. Fenton had always stayed with lace-up brown shoes; today's pair, well-polished and from a handmade line, were a bit worn at the heel. A pale-blue shirt was fresh from the local *lavanderia,* but a second neck button was missing and his sombre paisley tie was casually knotted with one end much longer than the other. Half an hour's attention from a woman would have transformed his appearance into that of an upmarket man-about-town. As it was, the overall effect was slight scruffiness, but with origins showing through.

The delighted taxi driver wrenched the suitcase from Fenton's grasp and glanced at the Hong Kong hotel destination scribbled on a label.

'*Dove andiamo?* Where we go sir?' The driver climbed

11

into the yellow Fiat, switched on the radio at high volume and drove away in the wrong direction. This irritated Fenton, especially as the question was largely superfluous.

'Fiumicino.'

'*Aeroporto?*' The voice tried to sound surprised.

'*Si,*' said Fenton quietly, and continued on in Italian, hamming the driver's own Calabria dialect. 'I'm running away from my wife – she has the radio blaring all day.'

The car slowed suddenly. The driver was confused at the flow of Italian from the back seat. Then he laughed, pulled the taxi over and backed it onto the pavement to do a U-turn. They moved off again, this time in the right direction, with the driver singing along moderately to a current hit. But after a glance at his passenger in the rear-vision mirror, he clicked the radio off.

'*Quindici mila – va bene?*' Fenton said, aiming to get the fare agreed. He pitched his offer a little lower than the driver might have hoped.

'*Si, si.*' The contract was grunted out. There was a moment's silence, then, over his shoulder, the driver added, 'They gunned down a lawyer at the Piazza Venezia today – lunchtime. He wasn't even anything to do with the trials. Those GAP[*] people, so they said. Don't understand it.'

'Yes, I heard,' said Fenton shortly. He could do without a conversation all the way to the airport.

'What do they want, these killers, *brigadisti* – Red Brigades, *Prima Linea*, the GAP and so on … What do they *want!*'

Fenton didn't answer and rustled open a copy of the second edition of the day's Communist-owned *Paese Sera* newspaper. Discouraged, the driver started whistling softly with some skill, and turned the radio on again – low.

The taxi-driver's rhetorical question, 'What do they want?' reflected of course the general dismay and incomprehension among an Italian public faced with a seemingly endless amount of terrorist violence. Fenton, as a

---

[*] *Gruppo d'Azione Populare* – Italian urban terrorist group.

journalist, sometimes had to write about it, and the question could have sparked a reaction from the back seat – if only out of taxi protocol. But the holiday mood was set, and after only a glance at the newspaper, he turned to thumbing through the pages of a Hong Kong tourist brochure offered by the travel agency a week earlier.

*

Fenton needed the break. It would be the first in a long time. Settled for the drive to Fiumicino airport, and basking in the holiday prospects, he jotted a few 'not-to-be-missed' notes in the Hong Kong brochure margins. His mind was far from Italian urban terrorists, but he was soon to discover at close quarters something of what the latter 'wanted' – and, more specifically, what the GAP would exact of *him*, Larry Fenton.

two

Hong Kong, 1978

L EE NEEDED to know that he was alone, or at least not being watched. The conditions did not make his task any easier. There was too much ambient movement, too much noise for even his trained senses to have much chance of detecting careful followers. The wind, the pounding of the sea on the shore and the hissing of the shingle being raked over by the back-run of the waves smothered other sounds.

According to the Hong Kong weather bulletins, severe tropical storm Brenda had arisen from a depression over the South China Sea. The morning after had seen the gale force winds dropping to a mostly moderate breeze. The sea, however, was still unsettled and every few seconds great rollers were crashing onto the foreshore of Deep Bay in the New Territories.

Lee stared at the sea again with a knowledgeable eye. The interrupted sunlight made it a quiltwork of jade and blue set in great, dull splashes of no real colour at all. Nothing. Not a boat of any kind was within view – nothing across several miles until the backdrop of the Bay that was the vague coast of Kwangtung Province in the People's Republic of China. He himself was a good swimmer – and acclaimed as such back home at the military base in Taiwan; he knew that even a young man, and very fit, would need a lot of luck with currents to swim that distance. A man in his sixties would surely need a boat, raft or some sort of support...

Patches of thin, swirling cloud bundled low across the sky; some were brilliantly white, others dark fragments torn off the earlier storm nimbus. In this ever-changing light pattern, one moment the rocky outcrops would be reflecting scorched white, then, suddenly, the contrast of hard shadow had scrambled the scene. And all the time, the tall sedges thrashed and swayed, and the flat clumps of scrub at the tideline trembled in the wind.

Lee continued his search, examining the storm-thrown flotsam as he went – sundry junk from both sides of the border. He passed timber pieces from long-lost wrecks and then, inexplicably, twisted bits of large trees in an area of coast where no real trees grew. There was also a scattering of tin cans, old light bulbs, bottles, the odd tyre and a number of rubbers of another kind. The shore was not exactly littered, but every fifty yards or so, some item made Lee pause an instant before moving on.

He had already covered two miles along the waterfront. Another one to go, and then he would meet up with a colleague working back along a similar, mirrored beat. They were part of a small team assigned in this way to search the Hong Kong stretch of Deep Bay. Four or five miles away, across the Bay, was mainland China.

In his early thirties, Lee was a strong, stocky man; he had a round, jovial face and semi crewcut hairstyle. He was fit, but the humid heat of the late morning made him sweat freely. A large patch of moisture darkened the back of his blue T-shirt, and he was continually lifting up the front to wipe his face.

In fact, he had walked a lot more than two miles. The navigable track was – in places – several hundred yards from the sea. Lee would leave his Honda 125 while he searched a section of the shore, and then return to ride further along; the machine always remained within easy running distance.

He was disciplined and dedicated, but he had not really believed anything would be found. Now, flagging a little and halfway through his task with no result, he even considered giving up. Reasonably assured, the easy option would be to make straight for the rendezvous point with his colleagues. With nothing to report, they could all then ride quietly back to Kowloon, and it wouldn't matter who was watching.

The thought was not followed through. Out to sea, something rising intermittently on the heavy swell caught Lee's attention. He felt a leap of excitement in his gut as he focussed his binoculars. However, what he saw was only a small raft of matted seaweed. Lee smiled. The incident was enough to put him back on course. He walked on towards a small inlet, by the side of which were the remains of an old, broken-up jetty spiking out of the shore.

Lee knew that his very presence in the area was unusual, and that it would excite curiosity. Several times already, as he made his way from the road or track down to the sea, people had spoken to him with more than polite interest. A worker on some irrigation project on the shore flat lands put down his shovel and asked where he was going. Then there was an old and bent Hakka woman garbed in black and carrying two buckets of cement on a pole across her shoulders; she had stopped, tipped back her wide-brimmed hat with its usual lampshade fringe and accosted Lee squarely with a derisive black-toothed smile. She, too, wanted to know what he was about. Nothing but a bit of a wayside demon, thought Lee, and earlier, the police jeep that had passed him on the track he took for a normal patrol.

But some of these encounters worried him. On a narrow path dividing great flats of water, farmed every year to produce a ton per acre of grey mullet and carp, a small, wiry character with metal-framed glasses and carrying a register-board put himself aggressively in Lee's way. Lee, speaking Cantonese, trotted out his story.

'Marine Department, Pollution Control Unit ...' Indeed, from his shoulder bag, he could have pulled out what for all the world looked like a set of bottles destined for an analytical chemist. It was plausible. But Lee's Cantonese had a strong northern accent; he originally came from Liaoning Province, and you can't get much further north than that without being Russian. He knew that on this of all days the accent would be noticed.

As he left the flats and scrambled up the rocky embankment that protected the cultivated area, he saw the thin Chinese with the register-board half running back towards a small shed that had a commanding view over the acres of fertile fishponds. Lee felt a flutter of alarm in his stomach as he noticed that there was a telephone line running from the hut.

He threaded his way through the gaunt stocks of the jetty. He stopped suddenly. Wrapped round an upright support was a huge jellyfish – several kilograms of gelatinous mass without form. Lee prodded at it tentatively with his foot, his face wrinkled in disgust. He couldn't tell whether the thing was dead or alive, but he did know that the tentacles of this species could sting dangerously long after clinical death – whatever that meant for a jellyfish.

He moved away, but after only a few steps, something else caught his eye. Twenty yards further along the shale, a swarm of brilliantly coloured butterflies lifted from behind a cluster of rocks like a handful of confetti.

He clambered round the rock mass, which was located at a low point near the surfline. He stopped abruptly, staring, when he found the cause of the butterflies' interest. A man wearing some sort of dark overalls was lying there, face down and stretched fully against the wall of hot white stone.

Lee rushed forward. A shower of butterflies took off again as he approached; he waved his arms in a half-panicky, half-angry gesture to disperse the cloud of fluttering yellow and orange. He bent down and in a fearful, minimum effort turned the head with short-cropped grey hair towards him. It was the face of a man aged about sixty. And it was the one they were looking for.

Still crouched down, Lee looked around quickly, wide-eyed and mouth hanging open in that startled, guilty way of those suddenly afraid of being caught at something. He could see nothing, and turned his attention to what had attracted the butterflies now hovering some feet above his head, buffeted and billowing in the wind in a strangely coherent cloud. He cursed violently. If he had been standing up waving a large coloured flag, the signal could scarcely have been more obvious.

There was nothing putrid about the injuries; the man had died some time during the last twelve hours. Nor was there any visible blood. The left leg had gone somewhere just above the knee. Lee couldn't see exactly in what manner it had been taken because the remaining tatters of the trouser material were stuck over the stump. It was the right side, facing the sun, which had drawn the attention of the butterflies. Most of the flesh from the buttock and down the back of the thigh was ripped away; parts of the pelvis and femur showed as dull, greyish streaks. What soft tissue was left had drained off and was washed free of blood.

Squeamish was not a word that could be applied to Lee, but he had to call on every reserve of will to complete his task. The leather had swollen a little in the water and Lee found his fingers fumbling desperately as he tried to undo the belt buckle. Seconds were lost in the common mixture of haste, fear and excitement.

He sat back for a moment, breathing deeply, with his fists clenched in an effort to summon the concentration required. He bent forward again and now with more science, more coaxing, he managed to slip the strap from the buckle. He pulled the belt free and held it up by one end for a few seconds in a brief gesture of triumph before slinging it round his waist.

With a last glance at the man's face – curiously relaxed, serene even – Lee set off again, half-crouched in an instinctive but inadequate attempt to remain unobserved. After ten paces he stopped, gazing at the gravel sand at his feet. Tiny shrimp-like creatures were seething and hopping around a dark, reddish-brown stain the size of a large saucepan lid. There was more of it a few yards away and, further on down towards the sea, a crowd of hermit crabs were scuttling round something that Lee did not want to examine more closely.

Again he looked back at the body. The man had

probably not died in the sea, Lee thought. The wounds, terrible though they were, would not have brought death immediately. He might have died from drowning or simply loss of blood – with the storm washing up the body. Lee concluded that the shark had not killed the man outright; despite the awful mauling, he had finally dragged his savaged body out of the sea to lie under the rocks. And if the tranquil facial expression was not just a foul medical joke, the man had probably died in some kind of peace believing that, after all, he had made the passage.

Lee was not much given to sentiment, but these reflections put a strained, tight expression on his face. For a moment he even forgot the urgency of his task. It was a lapse of only a few seconds.

*

He saw them coming when they were two hundred yards away, not quite running, but jogging with a purpose. One had the lower, surf-level approach, another was scampering across the rock-cluttered foreshore and a third was up on the embankment, barely visible among the close-hugging Sea Buckthorn scrub, which flowers camouflage green when it flowers at all.

Lee's heart jumped and his right hand went straight to his all-purpose shoulder bag. The first, instant, reflex then gave way to a split-second's reasoning: they too, were certainly armed. Three, perhaps more, against one were impossible odds, except in films.

He ran at full pelt. The nice dose of honest fear and certain exaltation thrust him over the three hundred yards with almost artificial ease.

Stamping the little Honda into life he took off along a track bordering a rice paddy lying fallow, which led to the bitumen road. In a quick look back, he saw four men running towards a black Mercedes Diesel 220D, which was already being spun around violently on the narrow track. One of the Chinese seemed to be beckoning to unseen helpers or perhaps he was just waving his arms about as people do when getting into a fray. Another was pointing directly at Lee and there was a lot of shouting, but at that range, no target practice.

A tight smile reflected his confidence so far – the car behind posed no real problem for him, certainly once he could reach the main Castle Peak road with its usual heavy traffic. Lee gunned the Honda, speeding through a small village without slowing. A mile or so later, turning onto the main road, he was satisfied that he was out of immediate danger, and he slowed to a normal cruising speed. Relieved of the problem of keeping the Honda steady on the uneven track, he could now think more clearly.

If earlier he had been the object of what the trade called passive surveillance, with which he could largely cope, he realised that since seizing the belt from a corpse on the Deep Bay foreshore, he was now under preventive surveillance. In everyday language, this meant a lot of people would soon be mobilised to stop him from delivering the belt.

The slower pace saved him. He managed to swerve out of the path of two oncoming Hong Kong Police Land Rovers with lights blazing; they were rounding a bend fast, and on the wrong side of the road. Could they really be getting out there so soon? Perhaps it had nothing to do with his business.

Lee was no fool. He had learned years ago that the hard-nosed opposition had huge resources; he stayed alert and observant when weaving through small clusters of habitation with disarming bands of children or livestock overflowing onto the road. He was paying more attention to the way ahead than to any vehicle behind. Even so, he saw the other motorcycle half hidden in the lush green verge a little too late. It was barely twenty yards away.

He accelerated immediately, hunching low on the frame. He had a fleeting image of the rider of the other machine leaning forward and propped against the handlebars, with a two-fisted pistol aim over the headlight.

Lee crouched almost flat on the tank.

He heard nothing, but a sharp pain burned through his left thigh. The Honda swerved, partly from the sudden violent reaction in Lee's body and partly from the clout of the .45 round that had the impact of a brick hurled from three yards.

For a brief moment the bike was driving itself and miraculously keeping to the road. Then Lee regained control. His left hand groped down the inside of his thigh and then pulled back quickly from the frightening, telltale wetness.

A moment's confusion made him drop speed suddenly. Not a trace of blood. But the hand was still soaked in some way, glistening for a second or two and then, abruptly, in the airstream, it had all gone and his hand was chilled. He shouted something in the wind – it was a cry both of provisional relief and of frustration. Lee looked down, but he couldn't see where the tank had been holed. Instinct told him to forge on. He opened the throttle again.

He had a good two hundred yards lead over what were now two motorcycles in pursuit, one of which had a pillion rider. No doubt the Mercedes was already lost, but now there was a more manoeuvrable team behind him, and Lee knew that a lot of other things would happen before he reached his Kowloon delivery point. How long would the leaking Honda last?

He grasped his leg, flexing it, and lifting it gently from the foot peg. Despite the tightness and the spread of dull pain, he could still move the leg a little. To Lee's surprise, a small open-top car overtook him, driven fast by a young Chinese woman. Despite everything, Lee noticed as she went by that the girl was beautiful and well-groomed, but at that pace, mindless. That casual thought made him reduce his own speed a little, all the while running through a list of options.

He was well practised with a pistol, but no real marksman. For some moments he toyed with the idea of going as far as he could until driven into the inevitable corner – or ditch – and fire fight. In fact the momentum of the chase urged such an honourable solution, and no further effort of imagination would be called for: the good soldier, under orders and geared up, dutifully blasting on until the end.

The shuddering rearview mirror told him that the first of the pursuers was now less than a hundred yards behind. He was still going at a good lick, but any faster would have been suicidal in the usual traffic on the twisting Castle Peak road, which followed the coast round to Kowloon city. He had seen grim government statistics to prove it.

Lee felt his leg becoming heavier and more difficult to move. The pain, dull and pulsing, was now generalised in the whole of his left side.

He suddenly had to swerve to avoid an elderly European woman wearing a large sun hat, pushing a bicycle up a slight incline on the road. The idea struck him there and then: a little further on was The Golden Park hotel, which catered for the cheaper end of the tourist market. Lee thought of the presence of foreign guests in the lobby area – a possible obstacle for his pursuers, and some sort of shield for him. This seemed a better scene than anything else likely to arise in the remaining seven miles to Kowloon. And he didn't know how much longer he or the machine, with its punctured tank, would hold out.

Moments later he carefully coaxed the bike up the short, curving driveway to the main entrance of the hotel. Lee hauled himself off the saddle, leaving the machine by the side of some waiting taxis. His movements were laboured. Apart from the straight-through bullet wound in his calf muscle, he had a sheared-off bolt and another flake of metal embedded in his left thigh. He stumbled his way to the main doors, slowly, like a drunk, with his head swimming. He glanced behind, down towards the road. His pursuers had arrived. An instant's pause, and then the bikes roared up the drive towards the entrance, with the gravel flying behind them.

In the lobby, Lee was seized by a dreadful sensation of

disaster and a lost cause. There were a score or more people milling around, but at first sight, they were Chinese of all sorts. Chinese, nothing but Chinese!

Lee faltered and all but collapsed then. His mind was blanked by both pain and smothering disappointment. Then suddenly, the noise filtered through his dimming senses. Many of the voices were Japanese! He was jerked back into reasoning.

He took it all in again. It still looked bad. He probably couldn't communicate with the Japanese. His tired eyes turned to the reception area where, in an argument with the clerk, were two middle-aged American women – also instantly dismissed as unapproachable. It was the end of the road.

He watched, aghast, as two of his Chinese pursuers raced into the hotel lobby entrance. Then he turned on hearing footsteps on the polished stone behind him. A tall, greying European pushed open the door of the restroom. Lee staggered forward and followed the man through the door.

three

IT WAS the advice of a journalist colleague back in Rome that led Larry Fenton to settle for the Golden Park Hotel. True, the place was thirty minutes' drive from Kowloon city, and farther still from Hong Kong Island, but it was half the price of the more central, internationally run palaces. And Fenton, on holiday, was footing the bill himself.

After a complete change of clothes – with an eye on the excitingly cheap laundry list behind the door – he felt ready to venture out into the Hong Kong scene. Already feeling the effects of the local humidity, he sank a third beer from the room drinks cabinet, and then walked down the two floors to the lobby.

The reception area was largely occupied by a Japanese tour group, all spectacles, straps and cameras, and looking only half at home. Fenton hoped that they were not all waiting for taxis. He hesitated. The intake of beer was having a natural result. He looked around the lobby for the convenience in question. It was identified by an odd sophistication – in a largely shirt-sleeved community: the common design of a top hat over a smouldering cigar.

Fenton pushed the door open and, through the vaguely comforting smell of the morning's disinfectant swill, he advanced towards one of the gleaming ceramic and chrome structures clamped to the wall. He was the only client.

Then he heard the door swing back again. A second later, irritated, he glanced at the other man who, breathing heavily, had slid into the adjacent partition; any one of the five other receptacles the newcomer could have chosen, better respecting a man's immediate territory.

'You speak English, sir?' The voice was weak, but only later would Fenton realise that there had been a despairing urgency in it. He didn't answer and looked away, or rather, down.

'American? British? Please tell me! Tell me, sir!' The Chinese was unbuckling his belt.

'Good God', thought Fenton. 'There's going to be some abominable scene – an oriental exhibition, even an assault! And I've only just arrived!'

'*Sir*!'

'I'm British,' Fenton said curtly. It was the first line of defence against aliens. Then suddenly the man was bundling the belt into Fenton's jacket pocket.

'Take it now, now to CNA – Central News Agency – or go to Hong Kong address. Second floor, number 42—'

The man stopped abruptly at the clatter of feet outside. He staggered back a few steps, one hand delving into his shoulder bag, but then he sagged and collapsed untidily on the floor. With shocked fascination, Fenton saw that there were small puddles and smears of blood all round the deodorised tiling where the man was sprawled.

The door was flung open violently. Three Chinese in neat, white short-sleeved shirts rushed in and paused for an instant, taking stock of the scene. The leading man was pointing around very deliberately from the washstands to the unoccupied WCs, to the urinals and then to Fenton, as if checking off an inventory. A finger was left pointing at Fenton accusingly.

'Police! You stay this hotel, mister?'

'Well, I came ... I got here today.' Fenton, stunned, looked mechanically at his watch. 'This morning – an hour or so ago.'

A fourth man arrived. Slim, well muscled, but bony above all; in particular, his elbows were almost twice the spread of his fist. He was somebody to avoid in a crowd. He stayed by the door. The finger-pointer swung round and looked inquiringly at him. The man with the elbows was staring at Fenton with careful appraisal.

Nobody, least of all these people, could have taken Larry Fenton for anything other than an astounded tourist. It suddenly occurred to Fenton that one of the others had a gun in his hand when they burst in, although there was no sign of it now.

The Chinese shook his head, almost derisively, muttered a sharp word in Mandarin, and the group hauled their unconscious compatriot out of the rest room quickly and efficiently – like ambulance men, but with a lot less concern for the victim.

Fenton stood for some seconds looking around, assuring himself that everybody had gone. It had all happened so quickly that he forgot that he'd had a belt thrust into his pocket. He turned back to finish what he had started and then went out into the lobby.

Everybody was still, hushed and looking outside. The Japanese tour group, herded together, had their eyes fixed on the last moments of what looked like a well-run arrest operation.

Fenton turned abruptly and went straight to the small bar in the lobby. A waiter detached himself immediately from a group of hotel staff and followed him.

'Yessir?'

'Whisky, please.'

His idea was to ask about all the fracas, but he had to wait while the barman prepared the drink with irritating precision. First the ice was thrashed into the appropriate size, olives and peanuts dispensed into separate bowls, and then finally the whole lot was pushed towards Fenton on a small breakfast tray. All he had wanted was a quick shot. The moments' wait had him musing. Back home, at this time, he would be sitting at his balcony-window desk, typing, with a glass to hand. He would look out over red-and-ochre rooftops towards the blackened bronze horses of the pair of *quadrigae* crowning what he considered to be Rome's most colossally vulgar masonry – the Victor Emmanuel 11 monument. But today, after a matter of hours, that picture postcard scene, familiar to Fenton for decades, had given way to a rumpus in the Gents of a cheap Hong Kong hotel.

'Well, after all,' he muttered to himself, 'I was looking

for a bit of a change ...'

He had barely touched the whisky, when there was another flutter of activity in the lobby. A number of khaki tunics of the uniformed element of the Hong Kong Police were clustered round the reception desk and the main doors. Taller than the others, a young British Inspector was talking to the duty manager.

Fenton left his drink, and edged his way up to the Englishman who was making a lot of bad-tempered north of Leeds noise. There was a moment of quiet, and Fenton got his word in.

'What was happening there?'

The policeman ignored him and continued to harangue the manager, mostly in English, but interspersed with fragments of what Fenton took to be Cantonese. The conversation was mainly to do with the morning's incident, but Fenton also picked up some comments over the visit of two particular call girls to the hotel a week earlier. He grinned and returned to the charge.

'Excuse me, sorry to interrupt, but what was all that about?'

The policeman glanced at him impatiently. 'Nothing to worry about, sir – nothing to concern you. Now step back.'

Squaring up to the manager again to continue his verbal assault, he had a sudden afterthought. Turning slightly towards Fenton, he added a reluctant and overcharged 'please', in deference to the European face.

At the same time, he seemed to notice a score or more of other people now huddled round the reception desk, all agog and listening for incomprehensible clues. He turned fully to face them and bellowed something short and brutal that sounded like a war cry to Fenton.

The audience of immobile oriental faces stared in interested silence at the uniform, and they edged a step closer. The youngish Englishman reddened slightly. He had a nice trim, fair moustache.

'They're Japanese,' volunteered Fenton, almost apologetically.

Fenton's expatriate compatriot glared, and then, with great spirit, snapped back: 'My Japanese has a heavy Cantonese accent!' For a second Fenton even liked the man.

The Japanese group's guide intervened, and the tourists, suddenly chattering and smiling among themselves, were led off to pile into a coach outside.

'Look,' said Fenton, 'I was around when they came in and got that guy ...'

He even had his hand fiddling in a pocket and prepared to haul out the mundane evidence. The policeman thumped both fists on the reception desk.

'*Everybody* was around!' He turned and gestured dismissively at the departing tour group. 'Now, just go about your business, sir, *please.*'

It was then that Larry Fenton made the decision that was to mark him for life. He left the bundled up belt in his pocket and returned to the bar. He was never sure, later, whether it had purely been the tone, the attitude of a harried and officious young British policeman or whether there was something else, even at that stage, subconsciously, that had made him hang on to the belt.

Without being asked, the waiter dribbled a little more from the Black Label bottle into Fenton's glass.

'Freshing it up, sir ...'

'That was a bit of scene,' remarked Fenton.

'Yeah, all over now. No problem. This is a quiet hotel.'

In his mid-twenties, the barman had the usual on-the-collar hairstyle, well-tended, and he was neatly dressed in the hotel uniform of closely striped brown jacket over black trousers. It was a good-looking face and honest, too, as far as Fenton could tell.

'Who were they?'

'You American?'

'British.'

'Ah, I went to London last year. My uncle got number one restaurant in Bayswater. Good business! My sister, she's nurse at St. Mary's Hospital. You call me Charlie,' he said, tapping the small name tag over his jacket pocket.

'Okay Charlie. What about that performance just now?'

The barman picked up half a dozen glasses in one hand and started drying them with quick, trade-wise movements.

'I don't know. The boys,' he nodded towards the lobby 'are talking about triads, gangs. I don't know.'

He arranged the glasses on a shelf behind the bar and then turned to Fenton again.

'We had a holdup here once – three years ago, soon after I started. But it was different. Lot of noise, panic everywhere, they firing guns a bit to frighten people. Almost funny afterwards.'

Charlie snatched up some more glasses with the same dexterity. 'You know, that time, well, it was all too ... too ... like simple?' He couldn't quite find the word he wanted.

'Crude?' suggested Fenton.

'That's it – that's what I meant!'

The Chinese bent forward over the bar and lowered his voice. 'But *that*, today – that was something else. The duty manager and cashier just sit down where they are. The telephone girl jammed the switchboard. I saw it – I was there and I sit down pretty quick too, over there on the luggage by the desk. Two of them had guns, but nobody saw anything much. They knew where to go. Only five of them, I think. Old Chan, the doorman – he suddenly wandered off and looked round the garden bar outside – why he do that? He's almost seventy, but still throws people out now and then.'

'Well, you saw it all – what do you make of it?'

The barman shook his head. He grinned. 'I live here. Got to be a bit careful,' he said, and his head arched round the building.

'Well, what was it?' Fenton persisted.

'Dunnosir, but it won't be what you see in tomorrow's papers.'

four

F ENTON WALKED slowly up to his room, unsure what to do. He was worried about the consequences of withholding information, and material, from the police. What happened here, in Hong Kong, in such a case? What did he risk? If somehow they found out, how could he explain it away?

Once in the room, he locked the door behind him. The belt, which he now looked at for the first time, seemed a very ordinary item. The leather was discoloured in patches like dried-out shoes after a soaking. There was evidently nothing special about the belt itself, and Fenton's guess was that if it was important it would only be because of the owner or because the belt signalled something. Should he go to Police Headquarters and claim that he had only discovered the belt after the event? Or perhaps he should find the CNA, whatever that was, as the Chinese guy wanted? That seemed to be the right move.

Fenton wore braces. Always startling – bright yellow or scarlet he favoured usually. The pair he had with him was an intense electric blue. It was the one flash of colour in an otherwise sober overall appearance.

He left the braces in place and threaded the belt into his waistband, smiling at what he considered to be a small piece of artistic logic. Had he seen the corpse that was wearing the belt, the idea might not have had the same appeal.

He returned to the lobby and used the pay phone to call the Foreign Correspondents' Club on Hong Kong Island.

'I want to speak to any British or American journalist who's around there, please.' On a sudden impulse and with inexplicable foresight, Fenton loaded his request with a strong Italian accent. It was a mild, not quite casual piece of deception.

'Wait, please. I'll try and see who's there.' The

receptionist's tone was polite, averagely disinterested, but it brought a result.

Through the receiver earpiece, Fenton heard some riotous laughter from several people, and somebody repeating more and more loudly while approaching the telephone, 'I'm very, very British' in a prissy, posh voice. First, there was a throaty sigh in the receiver and then, surprisingly: 'Jack Harper, *Sinny Mornerrol*. What can I do for you?'

It was the rough, indifferent snarl that Australians use when they're bored. Fenton grinned and went on with his piece, heavily accented.

'Sorry troubling you, I am Gioacchini, Italian journalist just arrived on a visit. I am working for *Espresso, Paese Sera, Manifesto, Grazia—*'

'Okay, sinyor, *okay!* Our wartrin-ole is dantan near the—'

'Can you tell me what the CNA is?' Fenton interrupted. 'A news agency?'

The accent on one side and blurred impatience on the other conspired to make a remarkable mistake.

'Jeez, you *have* just arrived, haven't you! That's the New China News Agency – Peking's buzz-shop. They don't have an ambassador, see, because they've always reckoned it's their territory, and anyway it's coming back to them soon ...' Jack Harper gave a short cackle of enjoyment.

Fenton hesitated. He knew that the Australian had had a glass in his hand for some time and probably there was nothing more useful to be said.

'Signor?'

'*Si?*'

'Get round 'ere, sport, and I'll tell you all about it. We'll find some Kyantee rewjo, or whatever!'

'Chianti rosso,' said Fenton, biting his lip.

'Right. Well, I don't think we've got any of that either – but there's the only beer worth the name – *Fosters!* Know that one, signor? Lots of it!'

'Thanks very much – *grazie mille*. Maybe I come

around soon. Thank you again, Signor Foster.'

As Fenton prepared to hang up, he heard Harper chuckling and moving away from the phone. 'An Eye-Tie with a bloody nerve – "Signor Foster!" Jeez ...'

If, for a few minutes, Fenton had enjoyed a factitious discussion with the apparently well-oiled Aussie, Jack Harper, the mood faded when he turned away from the telephone booth. At the reception desk was a police sergeant taking notes while talking to some of the staff. Fenton turned on his heel and went up to his room. Once inside, he immediately flopped on the bed.

He joined his hands behind his head and gazed at the newly plastered ceiling. With all the excitement, he had not felt any real lack of sleep or jet lag, but perhaps he should just doze off for a bit, get recharged. Fenton closed his eyes, but it didn't work. The day's events kept playing over in his mind.

He certainly wasn't going to deliver the belt to some official Chinese communist mission, which, according to the earthy Jack Harper, that Agency was all about. Then there was his gut reaction: why did he feel, in retrospect, some sympathy for the character who had pressed the belt on him? The outnumbered underdog maybe? At the time, he was almost glad to see the man dragged off and, for the moments that counted, accepted that it was the police in pursuit. Now, of course, he knew that it had nothing to do with the police – at least, not Hong Kong's police.

The four men that he had seen in the Gents were detached, in some way alien – not because they were Chinese, but in their manner. They seemed to belong to a different system, very assured and a law unto themselves. The barman had described it in his own way.

Before collapsing, what had that poor guy said? Fenton asked himself again. The man had been cut short by the arrival of the others, but the initials 'CNA' were clear enough, and he had even spelt it out: 'Central News Agency'.

'Good God ...' Fenton murmured aloud. He suddenly

leapt off the bed. 'Central News Agency' was not the NCNA – the New China News Agency so vividly described by Harper. Fenton cursed again. His normally precise way of thinking had been distracted, smothered perhaps by the Australian's colourful remarks. Fenton guessed right and found a telephone directory in the writing table drawer. 'CNA' was listed. He picked up the phone and dialled.

'Central News Agency ...'

The voice, Fenton thought, had a non-native American ring to it.

'Good afternoon. Quick question – do you take features?'

It was a vague, unlikely inquiry, but Fenton hoped that it would lead to enough conversation to tell him something about the CNA. He was right.

'You make mistake, sir. This is the official news agency of the Republic of China.'

Fenton swallowed in a suddenly dry throat.

'You mean Taiwan?'

'Of course, yes.' The tone now had an edge to it.

'Sorry. It's a misunderstanding. Thank you.'

Fenton moved across to the window. From that side of the hotel, the ground sloped away among groves of low trees, bamboo clumps and bushes, above which the tops of occasional buildings could be seen. Beyond that was the clearly urban waterfront area and, in the distance, across a gleaming strip of water, was the massive hump of Victoria Peak on Hong Kong Island. Fenton was staring at it all, but without seeing it.

He was shaken. There couldn't really have been anything worse than Harper's quick, albeit innocent, assumption that Fenton had asked about mainland China's NCNA when in reality it was the news bureau, Central News Agency – NCA – belonging to the fifteen million opposition Chinese Nationalists on Taiwan!

Fenton stood there pondering for some moments with his crossed arms wrapped around his shoulders. It all suggested a good news story somewhere, but he just didn't see how to get into it. And he didn't want to make another blunder.

In the small shower-room, he splashed some cold water on his face in a ritual attempt to clear his head. He emerged again wondering if it really was practical even to be thinking about making any inquiries himself. He was uncertain as to what there was to 'inquire' about, the local scene was wholly foreign to him, he knew nobody, and the chances were that he would get nowhere and end by making a fool of himself.

On the other hand, he had been witness to something out of the ordinary – a clue had even been thrust into his pocket. And, holiday or not, there *had* to be a story here – and one certainly a lot more spectacular than those he usually dealt with.

He pulled the belt free from his waist. He walked around, still undecided, agitated and swinging the belt like a sling. He was annoyed with himself. The telephone rang and made him jump.

He picked up the receiver. There was a click and a continuing buzzing noise. Then a voice broke in:

'Yes, sir – reception …?'

'But there was an incoming call for me.'

'One minute, sir ...' Fenton heard the hotel operator mutter something to a colleague. Then: 'Line was cut sir, maybe the party will call again.'

Already feeling edgy, the broken-off call made him even more uneasy. Was the call made to determine absence or presence? Fenton went to the door and double-locked it.

Then another thought made him catch his breath. The bleeding man they had carted off – they weren't being over-gentle with him even then. He was going to talk … Perhaps he had already done so. And what would he have been saying? That he had foisted a belt onto the easily identifiable European who was in the Gents at the moment in question!

For the first time in many years, Larry Fenton felt the pounce of real fear. He whipped the belt viciously on the bed cover in a rare show of bad temper. Being alarmed didn't sit well with him; moreover, none of the options looked right. Simply to deliver the belt to the Central News Agency seemed pointless – as far as his own interests were concerned. But he was certainly not going to give up. He decided that he needed advice, help from somebody.

The moment of anger passed. Fenton sat on the bed, thinking hard. He smoothed over the ridge that the blow had left in the bed cover. Then, studying the belt yet again, Fenton noticed something that made him stare more closely: stitching along one edge had split from the impact, and the dried-out leather had curled away in parts. The belt was lined.

It had never occurred to him that the belt could be a *vehicle* of sorts and not merely, as he assumed, a signal or sign of identity. He used a new blade from his Gillette dispenser to cut the rest of the stitching along the top edge. He found three sealed plastic sachets, each about eight inches long and as wide as a school ruler. Fenton opened one and discovered sections of 35mm film.

For a moment he thought that it was completely fogged. But close inspection against the light revealed the general form of printed pages – far too small to be read with the naked eye. The other two sachets contained similar film. Some sort of viewer was needed – and *presto*!

Most Hong Kong hotels have a reputation for service of all kinds. A call to the front desk was treated like a breakfast order. It was certainly not the first time such equipment had been asked for by a hotel guest – but for quite different reasons.

In less then ten minutes, a young Chinese boy had left the projector installed, properly focussed and with a specimen colour slide of the hotel facade thrown on the wall of the room. It was far from an ideal arrangement; Fenton had difficulty in controlling and focussing the unmounted negatives. But it was enough for him to see what he had got. He was confronted with fifteen frames of dense Chinese print, not a word of which could he read.

For a minute or two, he simply sat on the edge of the bed, staring at the apparatus, filled with a sense of despairing futility and frustration. Then he got up and padded around the room. Obvious ideas came to him. Filmed documents hidden in a belt that had been in water, probably the sea – by definition, it was something important. And that Chinese man in the Gents was not simply an accident victim – he had been wounded surely! Fenton tore up the plastic wrappings and flushed the pieces down the WC.

The dissected belt was another matter. It was a largely indestructible object, and it could still be relevant. It was not something to be left around – and certainly not worn, as he had cheerfully done earlier.

Fenton went to the windows. Luckily they were not battened down, as is often the case in air-conditioned buildings. On the wall outside, he found a superfluous nail that was painted over rather than having attracted the extra effort of being pulled out. It would suit his purpose nicely. He was warming to his task. Before leaving the belt hanging down by the buckle, Fenton wetted a finger, wiped it over the leather and put it to his tongue. The taste was unmistakeably salty. So, yes – it had been in the sea.

He turned to examine the negatives again. One, from its format, seemed to be the lead page. This frame Fenton cut away carefully from the strip and put it aside. Now shaken into a precise course of action, he was excited by what he had found. He was even beginning to enjoy himself.

He fiddled and poked around the room, trying to find a hiding place for the rest of the film. In the end he settled for the spine of the bound telephone directory. It was scarcely an original idea – no more than the belt hanging outside by the window. But Fenton was satisfied and found himself humming the E major bit of Vivaldi's tribute to nature – *Spring* – which he often did in moments of mild elation. He locked up and went downstairs again in search of the friendly barman whose uncle and sister were in London; there was something familiar, reassuring in that.

*

'Black Label, Mr Fenton?' Again there was that sudden flush of fright that made him catch his breath.

'How do you know my name?' he asked sharply. He hadn't signed any chits.

The barman hesitated only a second. He grinned. 'Over there ...' Charlie nodded towards the front desk. 'Only one Englishman comes in today. I asked. Sorry. No problem.' He grinned broadly again. 'I have to keep account, sir.'

Then Fenton realised that at the bar earlier he had drunk a couple of whiskies and, preoccupied, he had neither paid cash nor signed anything.

A Chinese and a European with a briefcase arrived and sat at the bar. Fenton picked up his glass, moved away, strolled around a bit and then placed himself at the end of the counter where Charlie had his operations base – sink, till and accounts.

'Look, Charlie, I need a bit of help.'

'Wait a minute. I fix this and come back.'

The smiling Chinese went off to the other end of the bar with two glasses and the usual trayful of cocktail extras.

Fenton's hand, sliding across the counter, half hid a $US20 note. The Chinese returned and the note disappeared.

'You wanna girl, sir? I fix something top class – you know, not ...'

Fenton was reminded in a flash that he had never been at close quarters with an Asian woman. He wouldn't make a point of it – even to intimate friends – but he cheerfully admitted to himself that it was at least an incidental factor in his reckoning to take a holiday in Hong Kong. He was periodically led into shallow adventures, after a painful divorce years ago, but in general had been successful in his resolution to avoid any further real emotional attachments.

There had been one exception – involving the wife of a well-known peer in industry. Although she, too, was subsequently divorced, Fenton had retreated and let the affair wind down. He had first met Joanna Waley during a visit she made to Italy accompanying her tycoon husband. He remained in wistful contact, and anyway heard of her often, as she was still an occasional actress and guest at TV panel games. Joanna had actually phoned him recently, with remembered warmth, about some family event of hers. Fenton sometimes wondered what the chances were – what it would take – to stoke up the affair again. However, for the moment, at the bar of a Hong Kong hotel, a proposition of a different order was ringing in his ears. 'You wanna girl, sir?'... Anyway, here and now, he was otherwise champing at the bit, and it was only for a second that he hesitated on the 'top class' offer.

'Could you come up to my room for ten minutes? I need some advice ... well, a bit of translation, actually.'

'Sure, Mr Fenton. I get somebody to watch here and I come.'

*

Charlie sat on the edge of the bed, squinting at the blurred, dancing rectangle on the wall.

'Not too clear,' he said, tromboning with his glasses. His head was weaving about like a boxer's. 'Leave there,' he said, 'I can see now.'

Fenton pulled his hands carefully away from the machine as if he had just put up a house of cards. He watched the other man intently.

First there was a frown. The lips were moving silently. Then the mouth of the Chinese formed a quivering oval; the eyes stared, and pouted cheeks let out a rush of breath.

'Where you get this, Mr Fenton? It's not good.'

'Just tell me what it's about – generally.' Fenton suddenly felt that he was being called on to increase the stake. 'Look, we agreed, you were going to give me some advice ...' He had another twenty dollar bill between his fingers.

He was wrong. The Chinese pushed the hand away,

shaking his head. His eyes were everywhere, and he looked alarmed.

'You give to police or maybe government. Or I do it for you. Bad stuff, this film ... You keep a long way outside! That's my advice.'

'Okay, Charlie,' said Fenton patiently, 'I take the point, but give me an idea of what it's all about.'

The eyes of the Chinese ranged over the room again. He got up quickly and put his head round the bathroom door. He scampered back, close to Fenton.

'I'm not talking to you, Mr Fenton. You journalist. You unnerstand?'

Charlie edged even closer. He was speaking in a near whisper. Fenton nodded. His face didn't show it, but he felt a bit vexed. 'Journalist?' The Chinese had read his hotel registration card.

'The slide – it's politics, or maybe army – says something about Chairman Mao.'

'But he's *dead*!' The retort came out like that, unthinking.

'It's politics.' Charlie shrugged and paced around, agitated. He didn't quite know what to do with himself. He sat down on the bed.

'Why do you say "army"?'

'Show me again, sir.' The Chinese wiped his eyes and replaced his black-rimmed glasses. Fenton clicked on the projector again.

'It's Ministry of Defence. It comes from the Ministry.'

'But what ... which Ministry? No, I mean where – Peking or Taiwan?'

'Beijing,' he said quickly, using the Chinese pronunciation. Then suddenly the Chinese frowned and seemed to be reflecting.

'How do you know that, Charlie?' said Fenton, sensing the uncertainty. 'It's written there?'

'Put on again, please.' The Chinese looked at the image on the wall for a second and then smiled ruefully.

'No, no address there. But it's the Chinese characters –

the writing. The characters are simple ones, short ones that only the communists use.'

'Okay, Charlie, thanks a lot – I won't forget this.' Fenton recovered the negative with care and slipped it into his wallet between some name cards.

'You forget very quick, please! Where you get, sir?'

Fenton ignored the question, but smiled reassuringly.

'Do you know a good translator, or agency?'

'I think about that. But if you have rest of that strip film, Mr Fenton, you get rid of it very quick – it's bad business. Not for journalists, sir, that's government affairs. Bad news, believe me.'

Fenton nodded and walked to the door to show his helper out. He was thinking that it could just be the best news that had ever come his way. If earlier he had been alarmed, frightened even, by grim evidence that the film itself was of some vital importance to others, all that was forgotten – for the moment.

*

One of these 'others' was Gerry Tan, well known in local business circles. Late on Tuesday morning, he answered a short and apparently anodyne call in his luxurious downtown office. He left immediately and went to the Garden Road Peak Tram station. There, he greeted another Chinese waiting among the small crowd. The latter was in his sixties, and a few years older than Tan. They didn't take the tram and, after a brief exchange, they both left. Tan was a top executive in Peeble Hunt, an old British firm in Hong Kong. This Cambridge-educated and prominent member of the Colony's social community, was an improbable party to be exercised by a washed-up body and missing strips of film. But he was more concerned, professionally, than anybody.

He was now grappling with the news that immediate control over the filmed document – a potential bombshell – had been lost. The document, as Tan knew only too well, was a shocking indictment of the late 'untouchable' Chairman Mao.

It detailed Mao's responsibility since the 1950s for the brutally 'radical' reform programmes and other appalling excesses that had caused the deaths of almost a tenth of China's population. By its very nature, the indictment, once in the public domain, carried with it the certainty of chaos in China where Mao for two generations had been God, and still was – to those who hadn't died under his policies.

As Tan headed back to the office, Peeble Hunt work was far from his mind. Instead his thoughts flashed back to a room in a Cambridge college twenty-three years earlier ...

five

Cambridge, 1955

'Odd thing. You know that I go along to these rather boozy sessions with De Vries …?'

Gerry Tan glanced up at his best friend, James Ma, who was brewing tea on a portable gas-ring in his college rooms.

'Yeah, too often – instead of training!' said James, with a grin.

'I mean … I suppose you know who he is?'

'Of course. He's that Dutch guy who comes down from London to waffle on about China, isn't he? The word is that he's a *lao peng-yu* – one of Mao's so-called "old friends". What's he done? Given up the bottle and gone back to join the comrades? Give me some more tea.'

The two young Chinese men with anglicised forenames were both from families long associated – through specific business or social ties – with western practices and culture. One of the families followed the defeated Nationalist government to Taiwan in 1949 when Mao took power on the mainland. The other, established in Hong Kong for a generation, had continuing close commercial links with China.

These eldest sons, from comfortable backgrounds, had thus spent their youth in different territories historically part of China proper, but five hundred miles apart.

They first crossed paths at Cambridge in 1953. James Ma, from Taiwan, had been 'released' by the military to study in the West under some vague Nationalist government sponsorship. Hong Kong-born Gerry Tan had got his place mainly through being exceptionally bright.

They were at different colleges and met out of a common interest in badminton, which, at the time, was anyway mostly dominated by Asians. They were both good players. A mundane dispute about the fall of a shuttlecock during one match fired the relationship; from then on, they were often together – on and off the court – and became close friends.

Gerry, reading law, was also attending some informal, extra-curricular talks on modern China given by a sixty-year-old Dutch academic with a certain flair. By way of charming the handful of devotees, he always brought along a highly popular self-service bottle of Dutch gin and a jar of pickled herrings.

Gerry poured the tea, and fixed his friend with a tolerant smile.

'Yes, well, I've spent quite a lot of time with old Genever De Vries over the last year—'

James Ma tut-tutted, wagging his finger.

'Well, you know ... after his talks, then drinks or whatever, chatting about events out there. Okay. A while ago he said he wanted me to meet somebody. And last Friday, he produced this guy, a Chinese, drifting down from London. Lu something ... Lu Te-yu, I think. Anyway, he was quite impressive – middle-aged, friendly, with a sort of easy confidence. So, we got talking, and our Mr Lu takes me off to The Lion for a beer – without De Vries. *And* guess what ...' Gerry paused for the punch line, '... he makes a pass at me!'

James Ma threw his arms in the air, and guffawed. 'You've been hiding it from me! Didn't know you came across like that!'

'Good. Glad you've had your fun. But it wasn't that kind of pass ...'

Gerry let it sink in, nodding his head, and poured tea for his friend.

'He knows my father, apparently. Anyway, James, that's beside the point. The crunch is this: Lu says that China is due to get the New Territories back in 1997, of course, when the lease runs out. Right?'

'Okay, okay – but it's the *pass* I want to hear about!'

'Just wait. He also says that China will extract an agreement from the UK to give up Hong Kong at the same time.'

'That's no doubt what they *want*, but even if the British did agree, it's a long way in the future – half a century away, almost!'

'Well, not quite … Lu maintains that China, one way or another, will get that agreement, signed and sealed, in the next twenty years or so – or "well within my lifetime" as he put it.'

'Where did he get *that* from? It's just speculation.'

'Not this guy, I think. But, listen, this is the best bit: he said that in the years to come, somebody like me on the ground could be a vital help in furthering China's long-term future.'

'Good God, he's trying to recruit you!' James was leaning forward, all ears. 'What does he want you to do?'

'Well … nothing.' Gerry shrugged. 'Just hoped that I would see out the course here, and then get a good job back in Hong Kong.'

'Come on, what about this "vital help" business?'

'No idea. Although he did say that the right, qualified people could look forward to senior posts in the China-run Hong Kong.'

'That's pretty obvious,' James broke in, then hesitated. 'Of course, depends how you take it, I suppose – it could also be a helluva big carrot! But what the devil does he want in return?'

Gerry Tan shrugged and shook his head. 'He didn't use their jargon with me, but from various other comments he made, I could tell he's well in with the Party hierarchy. But it was all pretty relaxed.'

'So what next?' said James Ma.

'He said he'd be in touch again. Anyway, it seems that he's spoken to my father recently. I'll call home and have a word there, to see what's going on.'

*

Over the next three years, Gerry Tan saw a lot of the man who called himself Lu. He listened to the latter attentively, not only out of traditional Chinese respect for age – Lu was in his sixties – but he also found the man oddly persuasive. Another important factor was the encouragement from his father, despite it being low-key and almost ritual.

The coaxing by Lu, skilfully applied, included, of course, an appeal to patriotism identified with a new, largely unified communist China. All this alone might just have tempted Gerry Tan to cooperate, despite the doubts he had. He was anyway hardly in the revolutionary mould; for better or worse, he was thoroughly westernised, had no particular interest in politics and enjoyed a lifestyle that, from one ideological point of view, was irretrievably bourgeois.

In fact, it was precisely Gerry Tan's public image that led Lu to persist with his cultivation. Because, in Lu's reckoning, *if* this eventual university graduate could be brought on board, he would be the perfect 'agent of influence' that Lu had earmarked him to become. Lu remained patient and understanding in the face of his target's hesitation.

A few months after the first meeting with Lu, the issue was suddenly settled. Feeling the pressure, it was inevitable that Gerry should confide in his friend, James Ma. At one point he summed it up as best he could.

'Call to duty and all that ... The whole thing is mindboggling. And, well, I actually *like* our comrade Lu – and De Vries for that matter. Very difficult ... But not sure I shouldn't just mention it to my tutor ...You know, perhaps warn him a bit about them. After all, what if the rest of the faithful—'

'No, don't do that,' James interrupted quickly. 'That's the last thing we want!'

'Why?'

'First, your tutor, old Baxter, is over the hill and wouldn't understand. And, second, I've got a better idea.'

In a rather heady and not unappealing atmosphere of conspiracy, the two spent several evenings talking over what was at stake. Then, within days, James introduced an older friend who was on a visit from Taiwan, one Sammy Lin. Gerry saw the latter three times that week; twice he was alone with him.

Sammy Lin had a different proposition, one perhaps where Gerry should have felt – if not through instinct, then by acquired inclination – on surer ground. After the earlier weeks of indecision, he finally bit the bullet. He saw no more of Sammy Lin at Cambridge. And he did continue to meet comrade Lu.

Moreover, Lu, acting as a sort of *ad hoc* and unusually benevolent travel agent, saw to it that Gerry's vacations, especially the long summer breaks, were in various places – including Hong Kong – and taken up with work. By the end of his four years at Cambridge, Gerry Tan had received as much, if not more, specialised training than was given to any new recruit in a Western intelligence service at the time.

*

In the following decades, back in Hong Kong, Gerry worked for several big companies and, from one move to the next, quickly rose to the most senior management levels.

James Ma finished his three years in economics and then went on to the Harvard Business School before returning to Taiwan to re-integrate in the military.

After Cambridge, much to the regret of both, Gerry and James – despite their habitual travel – saw one another only rarely, and then in exceptional circumstances.

Sammy Lin, James Ma's 'friend-on-a-visit-from-Taiwan', became installed in the 1960s as head of a Hong Kong Import Export concern. There, to those working closely with him, who were mainly Cantonese speakers, he was known as 'Uncle Lam.' He was somebody that Gerry *did* see, not often, but regularly, in what was no doubt the best-kept secret in Hong Kong.

Their most recent meeting, late one Tuesday morning in 1978, was at the Garden Road Peak Tram station.

And it had all started with the fall of a shuttlecock.

six

Hong Kong, 1978

THE BLACK Mercedes was left in a parking lot on the Hong Kong side of the harbour. The owner, who ran a small garage across the water in Kowloon, reported to the police only late in the day, as instructed, that the vehicle had been stolen.

The passengers, including the waterfront scavenger, Lee, were earlier deposited at a building in Pok Fu Lam Road at the western end of the Island. This detached three-storey house was a square, unexciting structure, not quite European in concept and finish, but still far removed from traditional Chinese tastes. It was the sort of place inhabited by Chinese with money who, for one reason or another, remained aloof from modern apartments or villa-type residences. The top floor windows, scarcely ever opened, were all draped with heavy net curtains. Individual air-conditioners ventilated the rooms throughout the year.

'Sit down. There's no point standing around and breathing alarm up here. Nobody should panic. We think first – then act.'

They were the words of a fifty-five-year-old Chinese. He wore no jacket; his handmade white shirt was set off by cufflinks and a club tie, black with silver motifs. His well-groomed grey hair was swept back and a small, neatly trimmed moustache added something extra to an already lined and wise-looking face.

He was Financial Director in the venerable British trading company, Peeble Hunt. This rare visit to the Pok Fu Lam residence had nothing to do with that. It concerned a higher calling. His name was G.T. Tan – Gerry Tan, to his friends.

He poured some hot water into a glass primed with

48

green tea and pushed it across a low table towards a thirty-year-old, who was wearing motorcyclist's boots.

'So ... You say he won't talk at all and has nothing on him – is that it?'

The younger man gestured with his hands, as if he were parting curtains.

'Only the .38,' he muttered.

He sipped at the tea noisily. His short-cropped hair exaggerated the angles of his head. He was slim, but quite muscular, and his large elbows showed prominently at the end of his short-sleeved shirt.

'I don't think it can be the British or Special Branch here,' Tan said. 'They'd have used more people and that poor chap would not have had to race halfway across the New Territories like that ...'

Tan's voice trailed off, as if he was thinking aloud. With his eyes in space, he was speaking Mandarin, larded with the odd English expression. 'Poor chap', for example. The other man had not understood, but he knew who was meant.

'The Russians ... I doubt that they have the resources here for that kind of thing. It might be the Americans ...' He was still musing, running through the possible options one at a time. 'But there again, they would have had more people and probably Special Branch as well.' Then he faced the messenger.

'How many were they – a dozen?'

'We observed four, perhaps five.'

The motorcyclist felt ill at ease. He cupped his hands round the glass, fingers fiddling with the plastic top that was supposed to stop the fragrance going off with the steam. He kept losing sight of the real problem and was already beginning to think defensively. It was Tan's whole manner and, not least, his way of talking that unnerved him.

'No, I think it must be the Taiwan mob,' said Tan quietly. He lit a cigarette. The other noticed, with instant disapproval, that it was from a gold-coloured European packet.

'That turtle Lam up there in number forty-two is

probably now, even now, in extraordinary conference – like us!' Tan leaned forward abruptly, peering intently at the other Chinese. 'You think that's so, my friend?'

'Friend' or not, he was seized by sudden anger. It flooded into him together with increasing incomprehension. Frivolity had no place here. He stood up abruptly, wrestling with texts he had half learned to the effect that problems should be addressed seriously in the light of the situation and –

'Sit down – we've got a job to do.' Tan's sharp but quiet injunction jerked the angry man into immediate submission. It was something to which he could respond.

'You are Shen, is that right?'

He nodded, surprised, and even a little grateful, flattered that the other man knew his name. He took heart.

'Give me half an hour,' Shen said. 'You know we have that room downstairs. I can get him to talk. You'll have the answers.' The tone was now bordering on enthusiastic.

Tan tapped out his cigarette in a large glass ashtray, and then slipped the butt into the Benson and Hedges packet. He sighed and looked at Shen with an expression so bland that the latter's nervousness returned at once.

'I saw him …' the voice was calm, measured '… round the door, as I came in this evening. Apart from his leg, his nose was bleeding and there were a lot of cuts on his face. One eye was completely closed. He was also holding his chest. Did he fall off his motorbike?'

Shen took a long, deep breath and stared at the accountant with ever-increasing dislike.

'Well, did he?'

'No.'

'So, he was softened up. What did he tell you?'

'Look, down there we can do things. I know I can do it.'

Tan stood up abruptly. A pair of rimless glasses had appeared on his nose. He was flicking through the pages of a small diary. He looked over his glasses at the very uncomfortable Shen, who was crouched on his chair and nursing a half-empty glass of now tepid tea.

'You are what is known in English as a bloody fool. Do you know what that means?'

'No.'

Tan walked towards a telephone placed on a small table under one of the humming air-conditioners, which was judged to be a primitive defence against bugging. In his hand was a small notepad, the pages of which had stuck together.

'Why was that man shot?' Tan said over his shoulder. His words were interspersed with huffing and blowing. 'The *target* was to be killed if necessary, so they said, but he was already dead, eaten by a shark. Why shoot the man with the evidence, the material? You had at least twenty people who could have gone along with the squad, and you know that you could have called up more ...'

Shen was in an abject posture with his head bent down and his hands dangling between his knees. It gave him an air of penitence that he didn't feel at all.

'Now do you know what bloody fool means?'

'No.'

Tan was dialling as he spoke. 'We have no local authority to go into that kind of interrogation – stage four, isn't it? And in any case, it has to be conducted by somebody qualified and in the presence of a medical official. There's nobody here and we would have to ask Canton, or even Beijing. It would take hours, days even. We don't have the time.'

The connection was made. 'Hello ...? Yes, Dr Fong, please ... Hello ... Yes, old friend ... Look, we have an urgent problem at the guest house.' Tan glanced at his watch. 'No, that's too late ... Okay, in half an hour, then.'

He returned to the table and studied Shen much in the way of a dog owner who wants to know if any real harm has been done to the whipped animal.

Shen unfolded himself into a more upright, interested position. Obviously he had misunderstood. They were getting a doctor around ... For him, the other man's style was full of ambiguities, and it was shamefully unorthodox.

'What about the motorcycle?' Tan was unsuccessfully trying to blow smoke rings from a newly lit cigarette. He turned to scowl briefly at the nearest air-conditioner.

'Unit three went out there about fifteen minutes after us. But the machine had disappeared.'

'Of course.' The tone was only slightly ironic.

'They are still there in case ... Well, it seemed to be correct deployment!' Shen sounded both defensive and anxious.

'That at least was good sense. Now, let's see if we can get a quick lead on the registration number ...'

Shen's mouth hung open; he suddenly looked shocked, almost frantic. Tan, misunderstanding the reaction, lent himself – with a bit of theatre, which he liked – to an explanation.

'Pouah!' he exclaimed with a throwaway flick of the hand. 'There are twenty-odd members of the Records Section at Hong Kong Police Headquarters – if we didn't have at least one of them, we would be failing in our duty. Don't you agree, friend Shen?'

He turned towards the telephone. 'So what's the bike's number? We'll get that moving immediately.'

Shen had one heavy elbow on his knee and he was rubbing his mouth with the back of his hand.

'We don't have the number,' he almost whispered. Tan stopped in his tracks. He turned slowly, walked back to the table and stubbed out his cigarette. He sat down. Shen realised that the other man had guessed the answer even before asking the question.

'You follow somebody for half an hour on the same bike, which is seen by how many others as it passed? You walk by the parked machine at the hotel, but you don't have the registration number?' The tone wasn't even sarcastic, which made it worse.

Shen stood up in some excitement and his chair fell over backwards. His fists were clenched white at his sides. He was exasperated.

'We were following the man! That was the most

important objective.'

Tan studied Shen for several seconds over his expensive bifocals. In a sort of slow wave, he removed the glasses, dangling one end of the delicate metal frames between his fingers. He motioned to Shen to sit down. This had no effect. The latter remained stiffly at attention, bristling with rage and impotence.

'It may not look like it,' said Tan almost casually, 'but I am extremely annoyed. My head is going to roll if this affair goes wrong – and it looks like doing exactly that. I shall be answerable not to the glorious Canton Command Unit, which launched a sort of vast air and sea expeditionary force – ludicrously futile and inappropriate – making the business even more conspicuous – but answerable to you know who ...'

He was wagging his finger at Shen who, although not liking units of the Peoples Liberation Army being spoken of so lightly, felt his temper subsiding. It was perhaps the idea that Tan's head might roll. He sat down again.

'Thank you. Moreover, here, with a general alert around the Hong Kong side of the Bay, and with all your manpower and resources, they – *they* find him first! Then what happens? Their operative rides round the New Territories for half an hour, gets shot – to attract everybody's attention – then he's beaten up. And what have we got? Nothing. So far it's been a remarkable performance!'

Tan paused and from a cheap kettle added some lukewarm water to his tea-glass. Shen stared at the floor, wringing his hands. He was afflicted by two reactions that went badly together: one of undisguised hate and the other of increasing humiliation.

'Bring him up here and we'll see if we can't find out what he did with it. If it's too late and it's in the wrong hands, there is going to be an international upheaval in due course and our chances of survival in that mess are not—'

'It's better downstairs in the basement.' Shen had not really been listening closely after the words 'find out what he did with it'.

'Bring him up here, please.'

Tan returned to the telephone. He was taller than most Chinese, with a slim, athletic build. He played several racket games well and had won a badminton half-blue at Cambridge. He still moved lightly.

Shen glared at the athletic back and his lips were tightly compressed like those of a trumpet player. He glanced at the two humming air-conditioners. At least that would help, he thought. He walked quickly from window to window to draw thick, dull curtains over the net ones. At the door, he looked back and saw that his tormenter was favouring him with a tolerant smile.

*

'Cigarette?'

Tan offered the packet as if this were any social occasion. But he was deeply concerned by the sudden turn of events. One new aspect that he didn't like at all was that he had seen this man before, in another place, in other circumstances.

Lee was propped up on a divan under one window. His good leg was cocked on the floor, the other one rested straight along the cushioning. He stretched his right hand towards the offered Benson & Hedges packet, then suddenly winced and changed hands. The little finger of his right hand, from the second joint, was bent grotesquely up and backwards. Before lighting the cigarette for Lee, Tan turned to look at Shen with a nodding, wide-eyed expression of mock admiration.

'It's the leg that needs most attention.'

If Tan had a certain style, Dr Fong looked like an average fifty-year-old local businessman – a bit overweight, balding black hair and with a brisk, energetic manner. He was from Hunan province where his name was really Fang; however, since moving to Hong Kong, he had learned that 'Fang' was inelegant – at least the way most Englishmen pronounced it – so he preferred to be called Fong.

'Let's have a look at the hand ...'

Even before he had finished speaking, he had folded his heavy black-framed glasses away into his shirt pocket, and taken hold of Lee's hand. In almost the same movement, he turned his body away from Lee's face, and then with his crooked forefinger and thumb, he pulled the dislocated finger straight, as if he were drawing a cork from a bottle. Lee yelped with pain and the cigarette dropped to the cheaply carpeted floor. Tan recovered it instantly and put it back to Lee's trembling lips.

The doctor had snapped his glasses on again and was busy with a narrow roll of elastic bandage to support the vividly discoloured and swollen finger, but which was now correctly aligned. After a quick survey of the other results of Lee's rough passage – mainly the leg wounds and battered face – everything was then patched up in a first-aid way, and a genuine-looking accident victim was lying there, astonished, still in pain, but feeling better and taking notice.

During the medical intervention, Tan had telephoned three times; once, a conversation evidently with a woman, had further sickened Shen, who had sat in stony silence throughout and looking everywhere except directly at Lee. The doctor packed up his bag.

'That's it. That's as much as I can do. There are one or two quite big fragments in the thigh and there's a straight-through puncture in the calf. He's lost some blood. Nothing really serious, but I can't do any more here. It's cleaned up, but it needs surgery to remove the metal and repair the tissue, otherwise he may be hobbling around for the rest of his life. Same thing with the facial cuts – needs stitching; it would heal, but with a lot of scarring. He may have a cracked rib, but I think it's only severe bruising. The finger is straight and ...' he paused and looked without smiling at Lee, '... the patient is conscious and grateful.'

Lee was certainly conscious; in a way he may even have been grateful, but it was incomprehension and amazement that his face most betrayed.

'What about the surgery, then?' asked Tan.

'Bring him to my place and I shall arrange it – or directly to the hospital. In any case, call me before seven-thirty this evening; I have to be at the hospital by eight.'

He went to the door and nodded perfunctorily to Shen who had turned to follow him downstairs. Shen wanted to make some telephone calls on his own account. His usual unit was under a different command, and he thought that a word there, complaint even, might give him some comfort.

'Stay here,' said Dr Fong, 'I don't need to be shown out. I know the way.'

Shen was not stupid, but he was conditioned; the voice of authority, in this case, medical authority, brought him to heel immediately. Tan drew up a squeaking rattan and bamboo chair and settled next to the divan.

'This will take less than five minutes,' he announced casually and offered the cigarettes again. Lee declined.

'Straight to the point, then.' It was the patient tone of the schoolmaster, assured and unassailable. 'We know who you are.'

Lee was staring at his foot at the other end of the divan, but he looked up immediately when Tan added, 'Uncle Lam down the road will be long since aware that one of his troops has failed to return. By now the news will be all round town, and Lam will have guessed why one man is missing. He probably even had witnesses to your ... your arrest. He will also have deduced that the operative in question had found what he was looking for. That's right, Shen, isn't it?'

He had flung the question over his shoulder at Shen, who was leaping up from one chair to another at the side of the room. Fuming and barely able to contain himself, his hands, too, were forever moving, twisting together, shooting his trouser thighs or clasped behind his back. He was very agitated indeed. He had never heard anything like it in his life.

'You were shot, rather unnecessarily, beaten up and then friend Shen here wanted to torture you.'

Shen ran several steps forward. His normally immobile

face was now twitching in several places from surplus emotion.

'We don't talk like that!' he raged.

'I do, and *I'm* in charge – not you! Sit down and shut up – or, if you can't do that, clear off and wait downstairs.'

Tan had scarcely raised his voice, but his gaze fixed the other man with cold intensity, in a remarkable demonstration of a commanding presence. A slight hesitation only, and then Shen again subsided in a chair. He was seething with silent outrage and hate. But there was the sapping awareness that he was out of his depth.

Lee, the other Chinese suffering for less complicated reasons, looked thoroughly frightened. Without being asked, he helped himself to another cigarette. As he tapped the packet, several spent butts fell onto the table. Tan muttered something, replaced the fag-ends and then lit Lee's cigarette with a slim, silver lighter.

'It is a matter of extreme importance, not only for China...' He hesitated. No, that was enough, he thought. 'We need to know now – and I mean now – where and how you disposed of the film. We will then get you to hospital. It's as simple as that.' Tan paused and studied Lee, as if assessing his weight.

'You're a northerner, aren't you? Where does your family come from?'

Until then, Lee had not spoken a word. He had no immediate family left on the mainland. It would not matter if he confirmed his origins – and the desire to speak after so long was overwhelming.

'We left Liaoning Province soon after I was born,' he said. Tan nodded.

'Well, to return to the problem, I want the answer now. If you don't talk, you will be put over the border tomorrow. You may even go back as far north as Liaoning, but not in the manner you would have liked. So let's have it – now!'

Lee's mouth had gone dry and his heart was pounding. He closed his eyes. He had reconciled himself to torture; he would have talked in the end of course, but he would have fought. There was even honour in facing death. But the possibility of being sent to China, had never crossed his mind. In such cases, it was as irrevocable as death but without the honour – being consigned to an ignominious oblivion, in addition to certain standard treatment for people like him. The mild-mannered man sitting by his side had known exactly where to apply the pressure.

Lee looked at Tan squarely with the one eye that wasn't closed. Disbelief. Impossibly conflicting ideas. He, too, had a good memory for faces. But it was Tan's awful threat that outweighed everything else.

'First, one question,' he said wearily.

'Well?'

'What film are you talking about?'

Tan stared at him for some seconds in genuine surprise. Then he looked over his shoulder at Shen who was standing, legs apart and hands behind his back, almost at the 'at-ease' but still 'on-parade' position.

'Sit down – again. And that's the last time!'

Tan pulled his own chair forward to confront Lee at closer range.

'You were observed taking a roll, a strip of film from the corpse at Deep Bay. You held it up – to have a look at it against the sky ... yes, *that* film.'

Lee, despite his fatigue, pain and dire predicament, actually smiled.

'It wasn't a roll of film. It was a belt that I took off him. I know nothing about any film, although I suppose there must have been something about the belt – otherwise ...'

Tan glanced round sharply at Shen who had his face in his hands.

'You should report what you see and not what you *think* you see.' He was about to add a more searching rebuke and then decided it was futile.

'What did you do with the belt?'

'I gave it to a foreigner at the hotel.'

'He met nobody,' Shen shouted. 'We were there – he had no time!'

Tan got up slowly, deliberately, and went across to Shen. His right palm whipped into Shen's face and as the head reacted in shock, bouncing back, it caught the much heavier, solid backhand blow on the other side of the face. The timing was perfect. Tan knew about timing from his racket games. Shen sat bolt upright, staring straight ahead and his hands were gripping the chair seat. Then, after a second he seemed to crumple, and he was nodding slightly in submission. Tan turned back to Lee.

'What foreigner?'

'Some English who was in the toilets, a visitor, must have been—'

'A tourist who arrived today – that's certain. I asked the man.' Shen wanted to get something right, although it had actually been one of his team who had spoken to Larry Fenton.

'What else?'

'I asked him to take the belt to the Central News Agency.'

'Why not directly to Uncle Lam's place or some other—'

'I had no time ...' Lee nodded at Shen '... *they* arrived.'

The rear legs of the chair creaked out a protest as Tan tilted back, distributing his weight unfairly. He coughed, took a large lungful of conditioned air and studied Lee's face for some seconds. He decided that he was telling the truth. He sprang out of the chair.

'You ... relax!' He was pointing to Lee. As he walked across the room, his hand swung round in Shen's direction. 'And *you* – get your senses together.'

Tan made an urgent phone call. He himself spoke very little, but the call lasted well over five minutes. Finally he turned to the others and addressed them in a matter-of-fact way.

'All normal over there, nobody unusual has been to the CNA today.'

Lee, in his misery, sighed inwardly, marvelling at the scope and penetration of their resources. Apparently his interrogator even had a quick line to the CNA – Taiwan's official news bureau!

The mainland's shadow fell everywhere in Hong Kong. A large proportion of its population had arrived from China, legally or not, since 1949. Moreover, the Communists' presence was widespread through official organisations like the New China News Agency and the Bank of China and, unofficially, through business and a myriad of other direct links with the mainland. It was a vast pool of resources where the word 'network' hardly seemed to apply; people like Shen and his group were everywhere. They were active not so much against British interests – they were more concerned with links to Taiwan, which was still, in the 1970s, committed to recovering the mainland.

Well aware of this, Lee was nevertheless shocked by Tan's bland announcement, which implied the presence of a communist agent even in Taiwan's local CNA office. For a moment, he actually forgot his own grim plight. Then he listened again. Tan was suddenly pacing around and banging fist into palm.

'It still looks bad, but it may not be too late. If he's gone to the police or government, we've got bargaining power, leverage.' He paused and stared at Shen – for no real reason – and then added, 'However, it's just possible that he hasn't done *anything* with it yet.'

He walked over to Shen and thumped him lightly on the shoulder. The latter flinched – unnecessarily.

'Maximum effort. Room, identification, contacts and blanket surveillance, but I don't want him frightened. You will *not* make any more mistakes. Direct action only if you're sure of getting the belt, or if he's passing it to somebody.'

The accountant looked at his watch again. 'In two hours, I'll have our other people mobilised – then it's back-up order for you!'

Shen nodded at the quickfire instructions. He was speechless, his mind numbed. True, Tan had got the Nationalist bandit to talk, but all this mention of *our other people* ... He knew this referred to a group of cadres trained in assault techniques and more. How could this man be stupid enough to refer to them in front of a Taiwan agent about to be released to go to hospital!

'What cars have we got downstairs?'

'An Austin Maestro and a Datsun 1200 – or we can bring back the bigger Austin.'

'Take him down – find a stick or something so that he can walk. One of the others can stay with him in the Datsun and wait for me. I've got some more calls to make. Then, Comrade Shen, you get that Englishman under control! No more mess, you understand?'

Shen nodded and hurried over to the door to shout for somebody to help him with Lee. They manoeuvred the injured man down three flights and then into the five-bay basement parking. Once Lee was installed in the car, Shen rushed off, determined to make his own calls.

Upstairs, Tan telephoned twice, speaking in Mandarin. He gathered up his suit coat ready to leave. He hesitated. Yes, he had almost forgotten. He went back to the telephone to make a third, very different call in English.

'This is Gerry Tan ... Put me through to Mr Hunt, please ... Hello Michael? Sorry to disturb you – surprised to find you still there – I'm not interrupting your shadow-boxing? ... Yes, I remember, Lloyds said they needed it by Thursday ... No, stupid thing, but I've got some sort of stomach bug. I'm at the doctor's ... No, but I've got to go for some tests tomorrow ... Not a week – a few days, that's all ... Oh, that's good. Okay, you'll tell them upstairs? Many thanks ... Sorry again ... bye.'

*

They didn't have far to go. Queen Mary hospital was just a short drive up Pok Fu Lam Road, heading west and among greener, less built-up surroundings. In the twilight, as the Datsun idled slowly past the vast, yellow brick complex set in pleasant grounds on a rise, both men stared at a huddle of police vehicles parked in the entrance forecourt.

'I can't take you up there all the way in this car. We'll go on for a minute. There's a bar-café further along on the right. They'll call a taxi for you.'

Simple precaution it seemed, but to the battered Lee, so close to release and the hospital haven, the delay also brought a further thump of anguish.

During the drive from the guesthouse, the strain was also building up in Gerry Tan; he felt trapped into a grim course of action that was profoundly abhorrent to him. He pulled up at the side of the road and stopped. 'We'll wait here a bit,' he said and switched off the ignition. He needed to take stock.

Lee, silent during the drive, desperately wanted to say something, to unburden himself. He had recognised Tan from another context, but he couldn't decide what that meant now. Unable to articulate the key question, he blurted out a compromise.

'Before coming to Hong Kong, I spent two years as one of the President's bodyguards. I once travelled with him to Korea.' He said it slowly, with emphasis, and he looked straight at the other man.

Tan nodded. Yes, Seoul was indeed where they had seen one another several years earlier. He felt his heart pounding; it made him shift a little in his seat and his face became set.

'What is your first name?' His tone soft and deliberate; he was trying to keep the tension from showing.

'Wei-min. I am Lee Wei-min.'

'Your family ... wife? Are they here or in Taiwan?'

'My wife died in a car accident two years ago. An aunt looks after the children in Taiwan.'

'Where? In Taipeh?

'No, Kaohsiung. Why are you asking me this?'

It was some seconds before Tan replied. 'Politeness,' he said, using a common, all-purpose Chinese phrase.

Yet again, his mind turned over the options. Only one would have the vital result. He knew he had to do it. It was awful, unbearable and, in the end, ruthless reasoning. Even if Lee wasn't abducted straight from the hospital, they – the others in Shen's unit – would soon run him down. It was not every day that a vulnerable and identified Taiwan agent was to hand. Lee would be interrogated, certainly tortured, and finally he would tell all he knew, before being executed. Shen's people were under another chain of command. If he, Tan, tried to intervene – even with *his* authority and standing, there would be imperative counter orders.

For both men, the phrase 'good memory for faces' had never meant more. In an appalling mischance, Lee, then simple Presidential bodyguard, had seen Tan at a bilateral Taiwan-South Korea intelligence briefing three years earlier in Seoul. They were together in the same room for less than a minute – while the President was being settled. But it was enough.

Gerry Tan leant back in the car seat, agonising over the awful reality. Details of the Seoul episode would soon be forcibly extracted from Lee. It meant Tan's real allegiance being revealed – with Taiwan then losing its uniquely placed and most valuable undercover asset. That was the crucial issue.

'Dr Fong, who saw you earlier, is a consultant up there,' Tan said, 'he's expecting you.' The tone was broken, anguished; he couldn't control it, but anyway Lee was hardly listening.

Tan restarted the car, drove on for half a mile and then gestured with his hand. 'There it is.'

A cluster of lights and a few primitive and unoccupied tables outside identified the bar. Its turnover must have been marginal because the area was sparsely inhabited – a few untidy shacks set back in sprawling vegetation. Tan stopped the car some fifty yards away.

'All right. You have some money?'

Lee, sitting awkwardly to remove the tension on his damaged leg, was deep in thought. He had to drag himself back to the moment. He shook his head.

'They kept everything at the house.'

His hand tightened on the thick bamboo stick that they had given him. It was solid and heavy, but there was nothing he could do with it in that confined space, even if he had been fully fit. And the other man, as Lee was well aware, was a very alert physical handful. He heard some coins jingle and the rustle of a note being thrust into the breast pocket of his shirt.

'You ask for Dr Fong, okay?'

Tan watched carefully as Lee opened the door and eased himself off the seat.

He staggered upright and looked down the road for an instant before walking slowly along the verge away from the car and towards the lights of the café. The movement was clumsy, one step at a time, then a pause and on again. He really needed a crutch and the stick was difficult to use. But he was mobile.

Tan started the engine. Then he slid over to the passenger seat and leaned out of the window. He prayed that Lee would not turn to face him. The man went stumbling on, without looking back.

There was intermittent traffic in both directions. Tan waited, chose the right moment and took aim with a German-made .22 target pistol set on a wooden butt moulded for the finger grips. It was modified to carry a ten-round magazine clip. He fired twice. Once would have been enough.

He felt sick. It took a massive effort of will, but he managed to drive quietly away. His intention to make sure that Lee Wei-min's family was well looked after back in Taiwan did nothing to prevent a surge of self-disgust that almost choked him.

seven

CHINESE POP SONGS all sounded the same, thought Fenton. The monotonous jerky rhythm and chortled half-notes delivered in a high-pitched, piping voice wafted from a corner of the dimly lit coffee-shop. It was a noise heard from every open doorway and window in Hong Kong.

His legs were bent up under a low table in one of the café's dozen miniature train-compartment cubicles. He shifted uncomfortably again as he tried to accommodate a bulky package between his feet. He felt out of place and obvious. Charlie, on the other hand, sitting opposite, seemed relaxed and at home.

It had taken a lot of talking to get the hotel barman to look at any more of the film; even the fifty dollars Fenton offered didn't count for much in this money-conscious city. Moreover, to Fenton's annoyance at what he saw as a senseless complication, Charlie insisted on meeting at this particular café in Kowloon city centre.

It was just after 10 a.m., and at this time of day the café, like its competitors, was mainly patronised by young Chinese. Of the score or more people there, only a couple of girls in jeans and come-on T-shirts stood out as being European. One reason for Charlie's obstinacy soon became clear. He looked both pleased and embarrassed when the young woman came to the table.

She was a twenty-year-old waitress, slim, pretty, dressed in a stark white cotton dress.

'May Ling,' announced Charlie with obvious pride. 'She's ... you know, she's my friend.'

Fenton didn't know whether shaking hands was called for or not. He started up into a preliminary crouch, banging his knees on the underside of the table.

'Don't bother, sit down, sit down, please!' She had a

ready smile and there was fun in her shining eyes.

The way she had pronounced even these few words suggested that she spoke English well – and certainly much better than Charlie. She went off to collect a beer for Fenton and tea, green and unadulterated, for her boyfriend.

Could it be simply the desire to show off May Ling that had motivated Charlie? Or was it, Fenton wondered, that the place and clientèle were familiar and that he felt more secure there? He made some polite comments about the girl and then drained his glass decisively.

'Where do we go, Charlie?'

'Okay, you follow me ...' He moved off towards the service door.

They made their way among pails of slops in a tiny, neon-lit kitchen area where an air-conditioner jammed into the wall droned and shuddered mournfully. Two bare-foot juveniles at a sink were flinging crockery and glasses about in a marginal form of washing-up.

They clambered up two flights of narrow stairs. The boards were broken in many places and old paintwork on the walls was covered in longstanding grime. An open window on the second landing let in the clamour from the street below; it did nothing to freshen the air, and a pervasive smell of kitchen waste remained, even here.

Charlie unlocked a door. It was a small room, with a wash basin in one corner. In contrast to the dingy access, the room looked neat and clean.

'May Ling's idea,' he said with a grin. This was evidently her lodging. Waitress she may have been, but these sparsely furnished quarters with a décor of posters and sundry bits of cultural flotsam, betrayed the occupant as a student of some kind. Fenton was pleased to note a Chinese–English dictionary on a shelf with a few other reference books.

He removed some bits and pieces from a small table and arranged the projector.

'Sit where you can see it best, and get yourself comfortable,' he said, drawing up a couple of chairs. 'I have a feeling this is going to take some time.'

Charlie got to work. Every so often he was scribbling on his hotel chit-pad. At first, Fenton had a flash of doubt.

'What's that for?' he said sharply.

'Some characters not easy. Different, you know? I write down – then I get it. Know what I mean?'

'Okay,' said Fenton. The young Chinese was trying hard. After an hour of listening to his rough translation, read out in fits and starts, Fenton knew that he had a front page story that would shock the world.

'I'll read back the notes – you stop me if it doesn't sound right.'

It was a good move. Charlie's comprehension of English was naturally better than his ability to speak it. They went through it together for another hour. The Chinese, with the help of May Ling's dictionary, frequently explained a point more fully or in a different way. At the end, Fenton was satisfied that he had a working summary.

'So, it's the Chinese Ministry of Defence. Right?'

'And others.' Charlie nodded.

He took off his glasses and wiped his aching eyes. The long concentration on a difficult text that bumped and danced on the wall and went out of focus at the edges had left his head swimming. He was wrung out, pushed to the limit. That was clear to Fenton. He didn't press further, although his face betrayed some impatience. Charlie sighed and massaged his eye sockets gently.

'Look, I ask May Ling to come up. Maybe she got good ideas – better study than me.'

'No, thanks,' said Fenton quickly. 'That's fine. I've got enough to work on.'

Fenton now guessed that the girlfriend's potential help was the real reason why they had spent two hot, uncomfortable hours in this small room. He glanced at his notes again.

'Just a last point, Charlie. One of the key issues – the Cultural Revolution ... I've got something jotted down here: "... murderous, mad policy and ... no difference between black and white". What does the last bit really mean?'

Charlie shook his head. 'That's what film says ... "*tsao bai pu fen*", I think it was.'

'Let's check the dictionary again – please show me the original Chinese phrase.'

Charlie thumbed through the pages and – with some hesitation – found the entry, leaving his finger on the spot.

'Ah ...' said Fenton, looking over Charlie's shoulder, '... "indiscriminate".' He scribbled down the word. 'We now have "a murderous, mad and *indiscriminate* policy". He smiled wryly at his ad hoc translator, and added: 'Sounds about right, I suppose, for the Cultural Revolution, Red Guards and so on ...'

Packing up the viewer, he lavished thanks and promised a generous reward, but a weary gesture of the hands suggested that the Chinese now wanted to be shot of the affair. From the word go, Fenton sensed that his helper, although evidently intrigued, was jumpy, and the brittle nervousness had grown as Charlie evidently became more aware of what he was dealing with.

Charlie led the way down again to the café premises. Watching Fenton leave, he wished that he had never become involved. He felt that he shouldn't have anything more to do with this Englishman and his extraordinary bits of film.

*

The hassle of watching over the rough-and-ready translation effort, left Larry Fenton with a need clear his head. To unwind, he decided to make for one of the landmarks he had listed to be visited – St John's Cathedral. The cross-harbour ferry and then a short taxi ride brought him to Hong Kong Central. But once there, in the church precincts, priorities had their way and Fenton found himself installed on a bench in the small garden. He began tidying up his notes, and the 'visit' aspect was soon forgotten.

After an hour or two of careful revision he was satisfied; he had a readable record of the morning's session. Excited, but wise enough to know that now, more than ever, he needed to lay off a bit, he spent the rest of the day as a tourist – ambling round Central, the cluttered side streets and markets. Sticking to western food, he had a late dinner in the Peninsula Hotel back on Kowloon side – another place on his list of landmarks to visit.

As he finished the meal, his thoughts returned to an unfortunate afternoon trip up The Peak. It had been something of a washout – no glorious panorama, no view at all. Thick low cloud or mist had obscured everything that was happening in the rest of Hong Kong below. 'As long as the fog stays up there,' said Fenton to himself.

His faint smile faded as a waiter brought the large bill. But it was, after all, The Peninsula, famous not least for being the place where the British formally surrendered Hong Kong to the Japanese in 1941.

Twenty minutes later he was back in his own, less illustrious hotel.

'Two-fourteen, please.'

The reception clerk handed Fenton the key, which was attached to a heavy postcard-sized piece of plastic – not the sort of thing you forget in a pocket. A handful of people were still idling in the lobby, even at 1 a.m.

One man was at the desk, leaning across it and apparently in a dispirited exchange with the clerk. Fenton couldn't see the face; it was sunk between the man's shoulders. His bare arms were laid out in front of him on the wooden counter as if he had just thumped it. He seemed to be closely examining the grain in the wood. Fenton, in good spirits, was about to make a facetious comment, but the blank stare of the clerk dissuaded him.

He crossed the lobby and passed by the bar. Two clients at a side table looked up at him with no particular interest. There was a new barman.

'Where's Charlie?' said Fenton, for the joy of asking.

'Off-time, tonight. Want drink sir?'

'No thanks.'

Fenton bounded up the stairs, two, three steps at a time. He was only a few paces from his room when he stopped abruptly. An image, barely registered a minute ago, suddenly coincided in his mind with another, earlier one, which had been more acutely perceived. The man downstairs at the desk, his arms, or elbows rather – they were huge on an averagely slim frame! Fenton had seen them before, that morning, in the Gents, adjoining the lobby.

At once, the gay, almost carefree feeling fled away. As he reached his room, the fear that had jumped on him earlier in the day came back. Something between panic and *bravura* made Fenton fling open the door with a brutal, decisive gesture.

The main light was on. That was perhaps normal. He locked the door and then stayed still, eyeing the scene. There was nothing obviously wrong. True, the bed looked a bit tuckered at the edges, and had he not left the telephone directory in a recess, rather than on top of the bedside locker? His suitcase was not quite straight as he thought he had left it on the low rattan rack.

He moved across the room to examine the case contents. Everything seemed to be there, although perhaps in less neat order than before. But an innocent room-maid shifting stuff around could have been responsible. One mirror door of the bathroom cabinet was fully open. The WC was trickling quietly because the cistern cover was slightly dislodged and had jammed the plunger. The brand new roll of toilet paper, which he had noted casually earlier, was now reduced, or replaced by something half the size.

Doubts plagued him and he couldn't be sure that he was not dreaming up fantasies to add melodramatic trappings to his journalistic ambition. But the evidence was there: the wounded Chinese who had approached him, the belt with the hidden film, the nice but clearly nervous hotel barman, his room somehow different, tampered with. The elbows downstairs ...

Very quickly he moved to pack up the portable typewriter. At the first tap on the carriage-return to square up the machine, the whole roller clattered off onto the table. Fenton jumped back as if the thing were about to explode. For a long time there had been a fault somewhere and the roller had always been tricky to replace. Somebody had taken it out. He was now convinced.

What should he do? Offload the affair – go straight to the police or continue to follow his adopted Roman nose for a once-in-a-lifetime scoop? Another factor weighed heavy – a sort of dread, a constraining fear of failure or of just plain fear. And that made him angry.

A few seconds' hesitation, then he snatched up his hat and dashed through to the small balcony.

Once outside, he forced the sliding windows closed again with the splayed fingers of both hands. With a small shock of grim satisfaction, he noted that the belt had gone from the nail on the wall. The next balcony, about two paces way, across a drop of forty feet, was directly above the flat porch way roof of the hotel entrance. Some piping, the thickness of a wine bottle, ran down the side of that balcony. Fenton thought that he could use it to scramble down to the porch roof. From there it was a mere ten-foot drop to the turf below.

He looked around. Two or three taxis were waiting in the driveway, and from at least two, Fenton could hear competing radio or cassette tunes blaring out. For the rest, it was quiet and there was nobody in the forecourt below. Fenton was no cat burglar or gymnast; he wasn't fit in the real athletic sense, but he was inspired.

He felt his way across to the next balcony by way of a ledge and then monkeyed down the gutter-shoot to the porch roof. He then landed on the lush turf with a soft thud and recovered his hat, which had arrived before him. The hat, a shapeless, narrow-brimmed affair of chestnut felt, was always a comfort, carried as often as worn. He walked quickly round by the blind side to one of the waiting cars.

The driver sat up suddenly from slouching over a

magazine, startled to find Fenton appearing at the wrong window. Fenton gave the only point of reference that he knew in Kowloon – Nathan Road, famous as a shopping centre and for its nightlife.

A quarter of an hour later, the taxi arrived in the area, which was still bright and busy at 1.30 a.m. Fenton paid off the driver and then mingled with a throng of all nationalities who were still idling in and out of bars, cafés and boutiques. He waited until the car was well away and then waved down another. Even for Fenton, not practised in everyday evasion, the change of car seemed an elementary precaution.

'Hong Kong side, Central District, please.'

He settled back in the taxi and a little spasm of excitement flashed up his spine; Larry Fenton was telling himself that it was simply a question of clear thinking. While the car was jinking through side streets to reach the harbour tunnel entrance, Fenton noticed the driver staring continually in the rearview mirror.

He squeezed himself further into the corner of the seat, but he couldn't escape the driver's gaze. What was unusual? Perhaps the ferries were still operating and that's the way most people would have made the journey from Nathan Road?

The car boomed into the mile-long tunnel. The narrow eyes of the driver were on him again. It annoyed Fenton and he was about to say something when the driver himself opened the conversation.

'I stop at Causeway Bay exit. You take another taxi, okay? I don't go to Central.'

'Why? What's the problem?' They were halfway through the tunnel.

'I stop the other side,' muttered the driver.

'What's the matter?' insisted Fenton. He was disconcerted at an apparent hitch in what he believed to be a fine getaway. He leaned forward. There was a sickly sweet smell of sesame oil on the plastic covering of the front seats. Did they really treat car furnishings like that – or had a recent fare thrown up? Fenton was not to be put off. He pushed himself back, away from the smell.

'Just why can't you take me to Central?' There was now some anger in his voice.

'We're being followed – I don't want no trouble.'

The Chinese spat out of the window and then fingered a cigarette to a mouth surrounded by scattered stubble that was not quite a beard.

Some quickly revealed instinct stopped Fenton from turning round to look out of the rear window. But again, the surge of sudden fear choked off his reaction and he could say nothing for some seconds. The acrid whiff of low-grade tobacco came around in the back of the cab immediately, together with some short-glowing fragments from the loosely packed cigarette.

Fenton crouched forward again.

'Listen, it's not the police – nothing like that.'

'I *know* not police.' The driver snorted out a nervous laugh. 'If police, me no problem!'

The car came out of the tunnel exit and swung round to join the main road leading downtown.

'I stop here.' The car slowed. Fenton wasn't listening. From his inside breast pocket he dragged out the first currency note that stuck to his nervous fingers – $50, which he dangled over the driver's shoulder. It was a great deal of money to be offering.

'Take me to Central District, stop when I tell you, and you can keep the change.'

The driver hesitated, rolling the cigarette from side to side in his mouth. Then in what seemed to be all one gesture, he threw the cigarette out of the window, snatched the note and changed gear. He was muttering to himself as the car accelerated violently, heading towards Central.

During the minutes that followed, Fenton managed to get across what he wanted. He wasn't sure that the driver was going to cooperate fully, but there was no real choice. In the heart of the tourist area, they took a sharp left turn at speed off a main thoroughfare, and then the car pulled up immediately.

The Chinese had earned his money. Fenton, prepared for the moment, slipped out of the taxi as if it were on fire. He didn't wait to see who it was behind. Indeed, with the area still cluttered with cars and people, he wouldn't have known what to look for until somebody pointed and shouted at him, or worse.

He half ran along a brightly lit shopping arcade, which led into a narrow side street. Gaudy neon signs announced any number of hotels. They all looked the sort that took clients with no luggage in the early hours of the morning for an hour or two. Fenton chose one more or less at random, although the name 'Victoria' had a vaguely comforting ring about it.

He fought off a moment of alarm on finding that the entrance was not direct, but by a lift set among a cluster of stores a little way back from the street. The hotel itself started on the first floor.

He took the lift up to the hotel lobby, and nothing happened to frighten him further. On arrival at the small reception desk, the duty man looked up from his newspaper and smiled.

'You have a room?'

'Yes sir, of course!' It was a cheerful reply at two in the morning. The clerk was already taking a key off a hook.

'Double, two persons ...?'

Fenton hesitated – for what any crook or spy on the run would call 'honest cover'. The clerk-broker weighed in: 'Short-time, double fixture, all night – no problem, sir.' He had an illustrated brochure in his hand ready for inspection.

'Just look, sir? Free to look.'

'No, not tonight,' said Fenton. 'Please give me a call at six – all right?'

A sharp, businesslike expression suddenly replaced the toothy smile and pimping eyes. Another man appeared at once and set about moving around already well-arranged items – a stack of receipts or bills, the telephone book, travel pamphlets and a small bowl of plastic flowers. He was watching Fenton. He was the second opinion, if ever one should be needed.

'Okay, you pay now – one hundred Hong Kong dollars.'

Fenton handed over a US $20 note.

The room was cramped. A partitioned-off corner hid a washstand and miniature shower system, the surrounds of which were encrusted with deposits so long in place that they no longer qualified as dirt.

A varnished plywood wardrobe stood in another corner and, apart from the bed, the only other furniture consisted of an upright chair and a simple dressing table. The air was hot and stale. Fenton pushed at the buttons of an air-conditioner sunk into one small window. There was no result. He threw open the other window, which gave him a view of a murky cluster of drains and piping climbing up the wall of the adjacent building.

The conditions scarcely entered into his reckoning. He breathed deeply at the window where the air seemed much the same as that in the room. He stripped to his underpants and flopped on the bed, his face relaxed, not far from revealing a smile. He had found a temporary haven.

Two days without sleep had its effect. There were some noises from the next room, which made him regret for a brief moment that he had not consulted the album of delights offered at the reception desk. The light was still on, but Fenton fell asleep almost at once.

eight

FENTON WAS WOKEN on time at 6 a.m. by a rap on the door and a voice announcing 'Morning call, Sir!' in a cheerful, sing-song way.

'Wait please.' He got up, grabbed some loose change and handed it to the boy at the door. Two minutes later, he was supplied with an electric razor – on loan – and a toothbrush set, unused. He cleaned up quickly, and at a little after 7 a.m. he left the Victoria and made straight for the Foreign Correspondents' Club.

The place was deserted except for a few of the permanent staff, one of whom had answered Fenton's telephone call the previous day and recognised the 'Italian'.

Once settled in the bureau area, Fenton took just over an hour to type out a tidy version of the take from his session with barman Charlie. Busy checking through his text, he was vaguely aware of the handful of pressmen who were now trickling in to read the Hong Kong dailies and agency despatches. One arrival he didn't notice at all – that of a well-dressed Chinese man, with suit coat casually slung over an arm.

One or two of the Club members would have recognised the formal striped tie, which was worn over a hand-made light blue poplin shirt. The general bearing of this Chinese announced somebody to be reckoned with. 'Accounts, book-keeping ...' Gerry Tan would understate on being asked his occupation. Never would he say Peeble Hunt's Financial Director, which was his proper title in the company.

In the corridor leading off from the bureau, he addressed himself to an employee of the Club. The exchange, which lasted several minutes, was within Fenton's earshot.

In practically any other language than Chinese, Fenton would have heard his name being referred to insistently. As it was, the tonal nature of Mandarin rendered the two syllables 'Fen-ton' unrecognisable among a lot of similar noises.

Looking back at the scattering of people in the bureau, Tan's eyes fell on the preoccupied Fenton. He turned again to the employee and asked who it was. He was told what the Club staff believed to be the case – that he was an Italian visitor. Tan hissed softly through set teeth. Something was wrong. The description fitted. It was true that they had lost Fenton late last night – lost, that is, within the limits of a few blocks. It had taken hours of laborious checking of all the possible lodging places in the area before an enquiry at the Victoria Hotel towards eight o'clock that morning revealed that the quarry had left earlier after asking directions for the Club. How could this Italian with a difficult to pronounce name – and looking just right – be in the very place where English Fenton should be?

Tan turned to leave. He was still convinced that the man at the typewriter was the one – whatever his name. He glanced at the Seiko watch on his left wrist: 9.20 a.m. It would take another hour to check back along the line.

On his way out, he passed through the bureau again. The folded suit coat had now slipped down the arm to cover his right hand. At the door, he turned slightly towards Fenton.

'*Buon giorno,*' he said with a smile.

It seemed to be an affable gesture, but the Chinese was ready to act on the expected response. Fenton looked up with a faint smile of appreciative amusement.

'*Sa parlare italiano lei* ...' Fenton was naturally disposed to be friendly – and here in the Club he could almost enjoy acting out his cover.

'*Quanto tempo e stato in Italia?*'

Tan felt a small a cuff of disappointment. 'That's too much for me,' he said, relaxing a bit. Then almost at once he reasoned that the fools had somehow simply got the name and nationality wrong. The man he sought simply *looked* like an Englishman. Everything else about the character in front of him fitted the description given. Tan set his teeth again and raised his free hand in casual farewell. Fenton smiled back, and then bent again to juggle with his text.

Little did Gerry Tan know that he had come within yards of the film that was so vital for him to recover. It was in an envelope in Fenton's jacket hanging neatly on the back of his chair.

Below, standing at the main entrance to the building, he hesitated. Somebody passed him and went towards the lift. Tan's mind was so focussed elsewhere that he failed to notice, in an unusual lapse for him, that the man bore a casual resemblance to the one he had just left.

He had a crucial decision to make. Despite the anomalies, his gut feeling told him that the European upstairs was the man to whom beachcomber Lee had passed the belt. Gerry Tan knew that he was risking his neck. He pulled a handkerchief from his coat pocket and wiped his nose.

Five nondescript people mingling with other passers-by took the gesture for what it meant: target on the premises, to be followed and taken if he leaves. Another, more extreme, course might have to be pursued, but they would wait longer on that; it involved an assault on the Club offices. For this option, a dozen other personnel were scattered around the building and two technicians were ready to deactivate a junction box fifty yards away, which had long been identified as the relay point for all telecommunications to and from the Club. Seconds later, a car with two men in the front pulled up beside Tan.

Gerry Tan, or G.T. Tan, as the name-plaque on his desk announced, slid quickly into the back seat of the ordinary but well cared-for Austin Maestro. He was going off to confirm his intimate conviction that Fenton was Gioachinni or vice versa. In fact, if he even got as far as the Golden Park registration card noting that Fenton had come from Rome – which small detail had not been relayed to him – the 'Italian' coincidence would be enough.

The running down of Fenton, the interrogation of Lee and indeed the whole initial border search were the sort of actions for which Gerry Tan was of course trained, and he had years of experience behind him. However, his main role was that of an *agent of influence* – a particular word in the ear of a Hong Kong or British official, or a piece of information or disinformation in the ear of another. This activity was so valued, and considered so sensitive by Beijing that for reasons of protection, street-level operations were rarely assigned to him, and only then in cases of exceptional importance. Recovery of the film, complicated by Fenton's interference, was one such case.

*

Larry Fenton, pleased with his progress, had just finished revising the first two pages of notes when there was a noise at the far end of the corridor.

'Line one up, Sunny, and we'll get the day started right.'

It was the unmistakeable voice that he had heard on the telephone the day before – that of the Australian, Jack Harper – confronting the Club barman. Then the voice continued, only slightly subdued: 'Hello, who's that?'

Fenton couldn't hear the reply, but suddenly there was an enthusiastic 'Ah ... Sin-YORE!' Harper was announcing his intentions.

Fenton cringed inwardly as he heard the footsteps approaching. He turned round and was dumbfounded.

It was no beefy butcher on holiday with a lot of muscular flesh filling a bush-walker shirt – as Fenton had imagined. The man was slim, and dressed in a light suit, much the same as Fenton's own, but newer. His general build was also similar and he was in his mid forties. Even their facial features had something in common: longish, well-drawn – although the Australian's nose was slightly more hawkish and the set of his jaw was heavier, more solid than Fenton's. His hair, too, was greying, but it had some

Brisbane sand in it.

'Hi Signor, I'm Jack Harper – been wanting to meet you since yesterday.'

He came forward with an outstretched hand. Fenton got up to shake it. He knew there would be an impact. It was a solid grip, but not, in the event, painful.

'*Si*, Gioachinni ... Carlo,' Fenton said, and smiled at the Australian.

'Right, Carlo, leave all that.' Harper gave a casual wave at the typewriter and paper. 'It's not important. Come on round the corner for a jug.'

'Yes, I have finished ... Thank you. But look, it's half-past nine in the morning – no drinks.'

'I'm inviting you to have a small *beer*, sport.' Harper had a hurt expression on his face and the tone suggested that beer didn't really count as drinks.

Harper went off brought back two half-tankards of Fosters Lager to Fenton's table and sat down. 'Okay, Carlo, welcome to Hong Kong.'

The glasses clinked. Fenton nodded, smiling, and more than a little embarrassed. He didn't like sitting at close cordial distance with somebody and all the while continuing with his Italian charade, but he couldn't see how to move out of it. And there was still some imprecise reasoning in the back of his mind that the longer he remained 'Italian' the better.

'Where can I get some good translation work done?'

Fenton didn't really think that Harper was a suitable person to ask, but he wanted to direct the conversation, to talk about something specific. He sensed trouble ahead with banal generalities.

'What sort of translation?'

'Well, it's Chinese material, a document, I mean – with a news story.'

'No problem. You can hawk it around the English language dailies – they've all got Chinese staff, translators. Where you start depends really on what the subject is.' Harper swallowed a third of the tankard in one go and then licked the froth from his mouth. 'I've been here six months, but they still won't let me drink it from the can,' he added cheerfully.

'No, I need first a translation – then I shall think about placing an article.'

While Fenton toyed with his glass, Harper lit up a pipe and made an effort with his hand to disperse the first pall of bluish smoke. He had seen Fenton wrinkling his nose.

Harper was mildly curious. The Italian's problem sounded unusual. He had arrived only the previous day, wanted to know what the NCNA was, then turned up at the Club going on about translation. It all prompted him to ask the obvious question.

'Well, Carlo boy, what's it all about?'

Fenton hesitated. He could hardly avoid an answer of some sort without looking coy.

'It's a China political thing.'

'Ah ...' said Harper in a tone suggesting that everything was now disappointingly clear. He sucked on his pipe.

'If it's China, you've got the *Far Eastern Economic Review* here.'

'What do you mean *here*? It's a British weekly, yes?'

'Well, no – it's published here in Hong Kong.'

'Is that so...?' mused Fenton. That magazine might indeed be a good place to start. It had a worldwide reputation and was often quoted in the international press where it enjoyed the labels 'respected' and 'usually well-informed.'

Fenton needed a friend, an accomplice. Could not the helpful, hearty Jack be won over into that sort of role? Earlier in the morning, Fenton had even considered getting out of Hong Kong. While shaving back in the Victoria, he had looked in the mirror and thought 'What are you getting yourself into, Larry?' In the end, he decided that it would be feeble and unprofessional simply to back off – despite the fear that came in fits and starts from the knowledge of being hunted.

Larry Fenton knew little about Australia; but of course

he had heard of Harper's paper, the *Sydney Morning Herald*. He had formed an obvious impression of the Australian: a friendly buffoon, open and who clearly had some experience of the local scene – here for six months, he had said.

'They're all right, the *Review*,' Harper was saying. 'They trumpet their wisdom a bit sometimes, for my taste, but ...'

He broke off as a barman appeared with two more half-pint tankards. Fenton had scarcely touched the first.

'Right, Sunny, thanks, leave it all there. I know some of them – the editor; he sinks a few now and then. I'll take you round there, sport; make introductions, if you like?'

Fenton made a further effort with the first beer. Maybe this was the chance to be taken. Before he could reply, the Australian asked, in a bored drawl, 'Anyway, emmachov this translation stuff is there?'

'Fifteen pages, small print,' said Fenton.

'Yeh, well, I suppose that's a bit of work ... Look, you don't need to push my nose in, but you've got something to say when you get round there? I mean—'

'*Si, si,*' said Fenton, 'I have a short summary.' He handed his two of pages of notes to the Australian. 'This will give you an idea.'

He could see no reason for not giving Harper a sight of the paper; they would anyway be talking about it in the *Review* offices. He thought that it was the right move if he was to seek real help from Harper.

For the first time that morning, the Australian put his glass down. He scanned the text, each hand holding a sheet and apparently reading the two simultaneously as if to recover his glass more quickly. He handed the papers back without any sign of interest in what he had been reading. Then he picked up his glass and emptied it.

The Australian glanced behind him, apparently in search of the barman, and then seemed to remember that he already had a re-fill in front of him. He took a mouthful and then there was a brief, screwed-up wince of doubt on his face.

'Well, Carlo my boy, that's a real speccy one. Jeez, you write better English than I do!'

'Speccy?'

'Yeh, well, it all looks like a bit of the old speculation. I mean, it depends, doesn't it, on who's saying that stuff you've got written there? If it's just amigo Carlo talking to a taxi driver ...'

'*Amico.*'

'Right. Then it won't get very far.'

Fenton laughed. 'Okay, I understand. In fact, it's a summary of a document – this one.' He held the three strips of film delicately in his fingers. The Australian looked blank.

'Is there a slide projector here?' asked Fenton

'Yep – round in the room next to the telephones. You can run through your home movies there, too – got any of those?'

'I would like to show you a bit of what this is about.'

They stood up. Harper took another swig at his glass and nudged at Fenton to do the same. 'They won't let you have tankards in there,' he said.

*

They found the apparatus already set up. Again, of course, it was not designed for unmounted lengths of negative film and Fenton had difficulty in getting the focus right. But he managed to push through enough frames from each strip to show Harper that it was indeed a fifteen-page document.

At one point Harper himself seized a strip and manipulated it through the projector himself, complaining that Fenton's hand wasn't what he called 'sober-steady' and even 'Sure you got it the right way up?'

They went back to the bar. At the table, Harper peered over his glass at Fenton.

'Lot of work, lot of work ...' He sighed. 'Anyway, drink up, Signor, and we'll step round the corner to see the boys of the *Review* if you want.'

Fenton put his nose in the tankard to show willing. Harper had already finished his, and stood up again. He glanced casually at his watch.

'Jeez – hold everything!' He studied his watch again. 'Look, I've got to go out for a quick ... It's, well, it's *personal* – you Italians know about that, right?' He had stretched his mouth into a theatrical leer. 'I don't want to lose this one. She'll be right if I just show my face for a few minutes. You stay here, finish your beer – and I'll be back in half an hour pronto. Then we'll shoot down the road to the *Review*. Okay?'

Jack Harper paused, looking down at the chair beside Fenton.

'Is that your beer-strainer, Carlo?'

'Cosa?'

'Your hat.'

'Si. Yes.'

Harper seized it gleefully. He rammed the brown felt on his head and clapped a pair of sunglasses to his eyes.

'The mafia attracts beautiful women, I think.'

He had reversed the pipe in his hand and was levelling it pistol-fashion at Fenton. In some sense it was impressive.

'I'll bring it back pronto, sport – won't even take it off!'

'Very Sicilia,' said Fenton a bit sourly. He didn't like seeing his hat leave. And as for the vision in front of him, it was a long way from anything Italian he had ever seen. In fact, apart from the minor detail of the pipe, Harper's general appearance resembled very much Fenton's own stubbornly Anglo-Saxon style.

The Australian, evidently fired-up, moved off quickly and Fenton last heard him telling the barman that he would be back in half an hour and to give the 'Eye-Tie' another beer on his account. Fenton sank back in his chair to bounce his eyes off his notes and to plot further.

*

'Mr Silverman, please.'

Jack Harper was using one of the two public telephones on the ground floor of the building that housed the Press Club. He was out of breath because he had raced downstairs.

'Hello ... Get yer nose out of the coffee mug and we'll meet under the trees, okay? ... No, eleven is too bloody late – you be there in twenty minutes! ... What? ... I don't give a *stuff* about the bloody conference – just be there. And ... Hello? ... Joe, my boy, you might even get promoted.'

He dashed out to the street and found a taxi to flag down. He got the taxi to cruise around aimlessly in the general area of the Botanic Gardens for ten minutes. By the time he had paid off the driver, he had jotted down a lot of notes in a sort of personal and chaotic shorthand meaningless to anybody but him.

*

'Nobody will let me get this goddamn report finished and nobody reads China economics anyway!'

Joe Silverman said it aloud although he was alone in his office. He plunged all his fingers into the typewriter keyboard and stood up.

He had been around in Asia for some years and was old enough to have been party to some not very glorious last days in Vietnam.

He pushed his head round the door of the adjoining room. The premature greying of his fair hair had not yet reached his carefully nurtured drooping moustache.

'Feedback is in a panic about something. You had better tell the front office, and also warn somebody in comms, in case we have to get something off quickly.'

One of the two secretaries ripped a sheet from her Olivetti with a rasp. The other blew a kiss. It didn't sound as if there was an alert.

'He's so insecure on the telephone, that sonofabitch ...' Silverman was muttering to himself as he walked quickly along a corridor with steel-protected walls leading to a side door of the building.

Known for his knack in handling difficult or forceful characters – the Australian, codenamed Feedback, for example – Silverman was also a careful operator. He took something small, black and unremarkable from General Motors out of the back parking area of the US Consulate General in Garden Road. The Botanic Gardens were only a short walk away, but he would never leave the Consulate on foot to go to such meetings.

He drove for half a mile to a roundabout and then doubled back before finally leaving the car in a side road near the entrance to the Gardens. It was illegal and he risked a ticket, but his was one of the professions where the fine could be charged to petty cash.

He went through the granite gateway, a memorial to Chinese who had died in British service during the two world wars. Continuing along the side of the central alley, he kept to the shade of the bordering row of flowering Delonix Regia trees. It was a still, hot day. Silverman had never been able to understand how the burning summer sun could leave the almost one hundred per cent humidity intact.

He was already wiping the sweat from his face. He could see a scattering of other visitors, glimpsed here and there between the lush clumps of ornamental shrubs and trees. It was strangely quiet. The vegetation in some way seemed to isolate the place from the general environmental mush of Hong Kong noise which, wherever you go, is never far away.

The smaller insects in the gardens were content with their anonymous fizzing and the larger ones hummed and fretted around the fragrant flowers of the shrubs. The only other immediately recognisable sounds came from the birds, the tropical sort that specialise in low, full-throated whistle calls and the hollow flute echoes of the disappearing jungle.

The scratching of Silverman's shoes on the gravel intruded on the softer sounds of the immediate background. Without really thinking about it, he moved off the path onto the grass verge where his feet were less in evidence.

Shortly before the fountain, the focal point of the seventeen-acre gardens, Silverman turned down an alley bordered by palms and Cypress conifers. He saw at once that the Australian was already there, sitting on a park bench in the shade some forty yards away; he seemed preoccupied and his head was turned in the opposite direction.

An easy smile appeared on Silverman's tanned face. The Aussie was an incorrigible clown. In a kind of exaggerated relaxation, his legs were stretched out fully, with the heels dug into the gravel in a wide V-sign. He was also wearing a crazy brown hat that Silverman had never seen before.

He walked on. But the Chaplinesque pose stayed as it was. Silverman's smile gradually faded. The man couldn't be drunk, surely – not at this hour! Then, with every step closer, he felt a vague prickle of alarm. Feedback was supposed to cross his legs to signal that everything was in order and that Silverman could join him on the bench. Nothing happened.

Quite suddenly, the tranquil atmosphere changed. The vivid colours splattered on a green backcloth were still there under the fierce sun, the insects droned on and the bird calls were imperative; but what had been idyllic became, in a matter of seconds, oppressive. It was a purely subjective change, of course, felt by Silverman as he approached the bench. It was the first time in six months that the Australian had not given whatever was the agreed signal for a meeting. Silverman's mind was automatically going through a checklist of possibilities. He didn't get far down the list.

In Vietnam, although Silverman had seen people dead, dying or actually being killed, as it happened, he had never before seen a man with his neck broken. As he passed the park bench, three yards away, the shunted, drooping position of Feedback's head made him stare, horrified. But his step didn't falter. He turned his eyes away from a particularly revolting detail: the Australian's pipe had been reversed, with the bowl in his mouth and the bent stem protruding from his bared teeth.

Silverman struggled to control the frantic thumping of his heart. Such were the disciplines of his trade that he walked on along a minor path at much the same pace for a whole seventy yards between the heavily scented shrubs that always attracted a host of colourful butterflies disguised as visiting flowers. He found another alley, which led back to the main gate.

Only when he was outside did he run. And then it was a panting sprint straight back to his office, with the car left to be recovered later by a minion.

nine

AFTER WAITING a whole hour at the Press Club, and with still no sign of the Australian, Fenton decided to act. He was not unduly perturbed. Although Harper had spoken of only thirty minutes' absence, Fenton just assumed that the girl friend was taking up more time than expected. For Harper, this would of course be more important than the problem of a lost Italian journalist all keyed up with some incomprehensible Chinese print and an unlikely story to go with it. Fenton was a bit put out about the hat, but he was sure that he would get it back eventually.

A short walk took him to the *Review*'s premises in a modern office block in the heart of Hong Kong. Fenton was agreeably surprised to find that the editor would give him a hearing at once.

'Well, what can I say?' Derek Campbell leant back in his chair and let the couple of pages drop on the desk. He was a balding fifty-year-old, with roundish features and a friendly manner. He gave a short laugh.

'You must know, as well as I do, Mr Gioachinni, that if this story is authentic it will be worldwide headlines and more ...' He shrugged and smiled at his visitor.

'The notes are based on an official Chinese document,' Fenton said. 'There is no question of speculation. It's official.'

'And in your possession? You have the original document?' Campbell steepled his fingers and looked intently across the desk.

Fenton fanned out the three strips of film onto the desk. Campbell bent forward to peer at the film, but he didn't touch it.

'I shall have to get my China staff to go through it.'

'*Momento*! I want—'

'No, listen to me carefully, Mr Gioachinni. This kind of

thing happens from time to time. Documents come flying around, picked up in a waste bin or something, and it usually turns out to be fabrication by Taiwan – the Chinese Nationalists – who go in for that sort of thing. Disruption, disinformation and so on ...'

It wasn't the first time that Campbell was smiling kindly at an innocent 'walk-in' with extravagant news that they'd just happened to come by.

'If you can be satisfied that the material is authentic, I want to write the story myself. You can guarantee me that much?' Fenton knew anyway that once he revealed how he had come by the film, and his subsequent experiences, there would be no doubt about authenticity.

Campbell scratched at his cheek and grimaced.

'Who did you say you write for in Italy?'

'I freelance around, the major dailies – *La Stampa, Il Tempo*—'

'You're a China specialist?'

'I arrived in Hong Kong yesterday.'

Campbell laughed and bit his lip. 'Look, Mr Gioachinni, my first guess – ninety per cent sure – is that it won't be genuine; but supposing it is, I'd do the best I can for you. No exclusive by-line; it would have to be presented with a lot of comment, we have our own style. Of course, you'd be properly credited, and in no sense ignored. We could give you—'

The door of the office swung open suddenly and a dark-haired European came in. He glanced nervously from the editor to the visitor and back again.

'But, you know, frankly, the material ...' Campbell opened his hands and shrugged. He turned to the newcomer.

'What is it?'

'We need at least another two columns.' He had a slight accent that Fenton couldn't place.

'Too late. It's buckled up for the week. What's so important, all of a sudden?'

'Jack Harper died this morning. Anderson at Police Headquarters telephoned to say he was doing us a favour by letting us know.'

The last, indifferent expression on Campbell's face froze with shock. He was silent and absolutely still for some seconds. Fenton also was seized up, staring into space.

'Good God,' murmured Campbell quietly. 'What was it – heart attack, stroke or something?'

The assistant looked pointedly at the visitor.

'Anderson said he was giving us first shot at the news, provided we just said "died".' He was making emphatic, soundless gestures behind Fenton's back.

'Okay, okay – he's a friend,' said Campbell quickly, nodding towards Fenton. 'So what happened?'

'Anderson says he was murdered – in the Botanic Gardens of all places, but we've got to sit on that.'

'Good God,' said Campbell again. He stared at the bearer of the news. 'What does Anderson want? I suppose it's the corruption thing we're doing ... Anyway, check back with the Commissioner's office. Er ... no, I'll do that myself in a minute.'

He paused and flicked through a sheaf of paper in front of him.

'All right, take out the piece on South Korea and I'll put something together before midday.'

The assistant rushed off and Campbell said 'Excuse me' to Fenton without looking at him. He made a quick telephone call to somebody at Arsenal Street Police Headquarters and received the confirmation he sought. He then pulled his attention back to Fenton.

'Good Lord! Are you all right?'

Campbell stood up quickly and walked round the desk to look at Fenton more closely. The colour had fled from the latter's face. Campbell poured a glass of water for him and put a friendly hand on his shoulder. A hand flapped a sign of thanks, and Campbell returned to his seat.

'That's Jack, Jack Harper – the journalist?' asked Fenton. His voice was hesitant and cracked. He gulped at the water.

'Yes, why – do you know him?' Campbell looked at

Fenton with renewed interest.

'I met him at the Club for a few minutes before coming here.' He had to make an effort to speak normally. He drank some more water.

'Why would you, the *Review*, be writing about him?'

'Ah, well, Harper was probably the best-informed of the China-watchers among the expats here ...'

It passed over Fenton's head, although the tone suggested that the *Review* didn't count as 'expatriate' and was in a separate category

'He was anyway by far the best Chinese linguist around. Tell me, what did you talk to him about before—'

'Jack ... Jack *Harper*, the Australian?' Fenton was appalled and strung out with fear, but it was mainly incredulity that his face betrayed.

'He spoke fluent *Chinese*?' he croaked.

'Yes, well, he had a certain manner about him, and it surprised some people. Before coming here, he spent – I don't know – three or four years in Peking for another paper. And before that even, quite a long time ago, he was teaching Chinese literature at the Australian National University.' Campbell was fidgeting with his hands, and impatience had accelerated his speech.

'So he spoke, and *read* Chinese?' Fenton asked.

'Yes, indeed! So what did you two talk about?'

There was a slight pause.

'Nothing much. We just chatted at the bar.'

Campbell was suddenly looking at him with real curiosity. Fenton sensed it immediately and realised that for some minutes he had been speaking ordinary, if emotional, English with no accent.

'Christ!' he said, and suddenly stood up. He couldn't cope any more. He put everything that counted away in the breast pocket of his jacket and offered a hand in farewell.

'I'm going to think about my China story and then maybe I'll come back to you later. Thanks for your trouble.'

If it had not been for an urgent addition on the death of Jack Harper for the current issue, perhaps Campbell would have tried to go further in discussion with Fenton then and there. As it was ... *arrivederci!*

*

As soon as Fenton had left, Campbell started pacing around the office. It seemed to be an agitated movement, but, for him, it was a habitual sign that his mind was concentrating fully. He was already rehearsing a text – necessarily bald, but a sincere tribute offered as much to an expert journalist in his field as to an occasional and valued contributor to the *Review* itself.

After a few minutes, Campbell landed in his desk chair again and he was ready to go. He reached for a sheet of paper to feed the machine. He cursed as the brisk gesture knocked over Fenton's glass. He hesitated. Yes, that, after all, was another matter that needed sorting out. He picked up an inter-office phone and spoke to his man who looked after regional affairs.

'Ted, who do we know in Rome?' There was a slight pause as Ted worked round to the precise sense of the question.

'Well, there's that guy Denis Miller who sends us a few pieces now and then.'

'Call him! And if that doesn't work, if he's no longer there, try Reuters. I don't care who you get out of bed, but I want a five-line rundown on an Italian journalist speaking virtually bilingual English called Carlo Gioachinni ... Yes, It's spelt with two Ns ... Quid pro quo – they owe us a bit.'

Campbell bent to the typewriter: 'A colleague's death has more ...' Then he stopped. He clasped his hands behind his head and leaned back in the chair for a few moments of reflection – irrelevant to his sad and necessarily limited copy to appear in the morning.

'Why would anybody,' he said aloud, 'want to kill that big-hearted, talented, super-nice man, Jack Harper?'

ten

A FTER A SHORT buzzing noise, there was a click, and the steel grille door swung open. A US Marine guard had a register pad open on his desk. These sentinels at American embassies round the world seem to be chosen because they all look as if they have a platoon behind them.

It's the uniform, of course – the idea of reinforcements around the corner. The security is more obviously elaborate in certain confrontation areas. Most of the time, Grosvenor Square, London W1, is not really in that category, but the Embassy premises bristle with as much protection as anywhere.

'I'll just look at your briefcase, sir.'

It was the second check since entering the building. The well-groomed and thickly-built Chinese flicked at the catches on the case and pulled the cover up. The guard satisfied himself about the contents: electric razor, toothbrush, several papers and magazines, a tube of Tiger Balm balsam and pills that some travellers are never without. He closed the case and handed it back.

'Please wait over there.'

At the second checkpoint, the Chinese had not given his name. Instead, he had written a brief note under the eye of the guard, and addressed it to an official in the Embassy, Lou Appleton. The visitor had spoken perfect English, and the guard could have been excused for taking him for a US citizen.

He moved towards the small reception area indicated. He had sat for barely a minute when a thirty-year-old man, relaxed in shirtsleeves, but with a neat tie, arrived with a 'Follow me, please.'

It took another two minutes moving up to a higher floor and through several combination-locked doors and grilles before they arrived at the office of the CIA's Chief of Station in London.

The relatively modest rank of Air Force Colonel belied James Ma's real authority and competence. He was a Deputy Director of the National Security Bureau (NSB) in Taiwan; he was also head of the Plans Division of that Service, which meant that he was effectively in charge of all the Nationalists' offensive intelligence operations.

Physically he was a tough, sturdy little man and a two-time survivor of largely unsuccessful sabotage operations against mainland China when Taiwan was still doing that sort of thing. His perfect American English was only partly due to long association with the CIA; in earlier times he had also graduated from Harvard Business School. Before that, he was in the UK for three years, studying at Cambridge University, also at the military's expense.

Lou Appleton had listened without interruption for twenty minutes. A huge man, with a fissured tree stump of a face crowned with close-cropped grey hair, he was a little overweight, but given his general size, it wasn't that noticeable. He had three sheets of paper in front of him on each of which in turn he was jotting down notes as James Ma talked.

There was a pause. Appleton looked over his gold-framed glasses. The desk was uncluttered. There was only one telephone and an inter-office press-button communications system.

'Fascinating, Jimmy, fascinating.'

Appleton had an unlit pipe continually travelling from one corner of his mouth to the other – one sure sign of a redeemed cigarette smoker. He had a soft voice, but coming from that bulk, people listened carefully.

'I've pulled a few questions out of all this ...' His eyes roved over the sheets on the desk. 'Here we go: first, that man of yours – Lee, wasn't it, was killed with small-bore accuracy in Hong Kong, right? How do you know they didn't actually recover the film from him?'

'Because out there, the Chicoms are running around in

bigger and bigger circles. And anyway we ...' He hesitated. 'No, we're sure the Fenton guy had it – and probably still does.'

'Yes, I was coming to that – how the hell do you know this Fenton got it?'

Ma scratched his nose with the crook of his index finger. It was a moment before he replied.

'We've lost one to a shark, but he wasn't our only highly placed source. In short, it comes from ... well, it comes from Peking. It's a hundred per cent sure. Believe me, Lou.'

Appleton studied the Chinese for a second.

'Congratulations,' he said, and the cracks in his bark-like face deepened into a wry smile. Then he snapped the pipe from his mouth and the smile went with it.

'Fenton. How is it possible that they haven't found him? You know as well as I do that no European can disappear in Hong Kong – without help – for more than a few hours. Is he working for somebody?'

'Good question. Could be the Brits, or maybe even the Italians – I think they've got a couple of people in Hong Kong. Never mind. Here's a bit extra – the bit that counts. Yesterday ...' Ma stopped and then corrected himself. 'No, the day before, an Australian journalist was found murdered in the Botanical Gardens.'

'"Botanic" is the weird official name. And what's that got to do—'

'Listen, will you, Lou? We have it that he looked very much like our friend Fenton – his general appearance ...'

Appleton mulled that over and went on listening, as advised, waiting for the rest.

'Also, he was wearing Fenton's hat when he was killed.'

For an instant Appleton's eyes opened wide over his glasses. Then he grunted out a short laugh.

'Yeah, it could be funny,' said the Chinese evenly, 'but the man died.'

Appleton stroked his chin with the top of the pen.

'That's very precise information, Jimmy – I mean, the *hat...*?' he said slowly.

Ma shrugged. 'Everybody has a friend in Hong Kong Special Branch.'

Appleton arched his eyebrows and sighed.

'You probably at least know the name,' Jimmy Ma added. 'He was what you might call an old China hand – Jack Harper.'

The American's head jerked slightly and then he was quite still for a few seconds, staring at his visitor. Then he thrust the pipe back in his mouth.

'Yes,' he said, 'I've heard of him.'

As it happened, he could have elaborated a great deal. Appleton himself had spent many years on the China circuit in Hong Kong, Taiwan and parts of South East Asia; it had never been his case, but he had long since guessed that the agent known as 'Feedback' had been none other than the improbable Jack Harper.

'So, it appears they mistook Harper for Fenton?'

'We're sure! He was taken out. In fact his neck was broken – we've seen it before. You remember the Suslov case? There's only one conclusion.'

'What the devil was Harper doing with Fenton's hat?'

'*That...* Anybody's guess. But it's certain. Not only casual, visual opinion – the goddamn name was marked in the sweatband!'

'Jimmy, look, let's check the loose ends.' Appleton was scribbling something as he spoke. 'Nothing unusual out of Hong Kong in the last few days. How come there's no big news that Peking's Deputy Chief of Staff – General Lin, for God's sake – was washed up on a Hong Kong beach?'

'Hah, my guess – yours too, I bet – is that the British, the Hong Kong Government, hope that if they keep the wraps on what to everybody looks like a would-be, high-level defection, they can avoid upsetting the Chicoms – let's not rock the Peking boat!'

Colonel Jimmy Ma was bitter, and delivered the last phrase with an exaggerated English accent that even made

Appleton wince.

'They've identified him, all right,' Ma continued. 'First there was a normal police patrol, but after that, it was all round-eyes.'

'Come on, it's a really good haul. I don't understand. The Brits may be cautious, but they're not going to sit on something like that without telling us.'

'It's not the point, Lou.' Ma was pounding his knee with a fist. 'Never mind what they're doing about the body. It's the material he was bringing out that really counts.'

Appleton habitually wrote with his head well away from the paper. He was taking notes, but the small movements of the pen in his great claw of a hand were hardly noticeable. His heavy eyelids lifted and he looked again, very straight, at the Chinese over the frames of his glasses.

'Let's get to the material later. But first, you know that we can't do much in Hong Kong to find Fenton without British help. You've come to London – why didn't you go directly to MI6? You know where they live.'

'Aw, come off it, Lou.' It was a sort of impatient growl, but the face of the Chinese had set into a tight grin. 'Before Kissinger, we could have done it. But now? Anyway, I knew you were here; you have the China background, and we both know that the Agency has clout with the British that we haven't got.'

'Yes,' said Appleton quietly, and he underlined something on one of his pages. 'Tell me, why should General Lin, one of the inner circle, have wanted to break out now?'

'We don't know the real details. We'd been in touch with him for years, almost a working lifetime. But he blew the evacuation whistle, and we did what we could. It wasn't quite enough. My own guess is that it wasn't directly concerned with the indictment – and it's *that* I'm really here about.'

'Right. We're there now. What is it? What indictment?'

'The material, the film – I'm getting to it. Just listen. Something evidently was going wrong for Lin, and he feared he was about to be blown, put away perhaps. Anyway, he'd earlier managed to give us a brief outline, but the whole thing – this indictment – was on film. Our last message to him was to forget the Order of Battle stuff and focus on bringing out the film, if he could bring anything at all. I now wish we hadn't sent that message.'

'How come?' Appleton sat very still, his eyes fixed on the visitor.

Jimmy Ma stared down at his finger tips tapping together: 'If word of this session ever gets back, I'll be put against that Taipeh Garrison wall – no trial, nothing polite like that.'

'You know that you can count on us, our—'

Ma pushed his open palms towards the American to cut off largely meaningless assurances.

'Well, this is the crunch. I had better tell you. We reckoned that only one of three things could happen: one, we get the film; two, the film is destroyed and then, three, they somehow get the thing back. In the event, it's out of control – the unforeseen happens: an outside third party, this hack Fenton, screws it up! And that's bad, Lou, believe me, very bad. It's the scenario for the next war ...' Ma broke off and lit a cigarette.

Appleton leaned back in his chair, waiting and patient. He had known Jimmy Ma for a long time and he guessed that the Chinese wanted to choose his words carefully.

'This document, what I'm calling the 'indictment' – it's not simply a bit more debunking of Mao. It rewrites history. The paper treats him virtually as a mad criminal foisted on a quarter of the world's population for thirty years. The Khrushchev attack on Stalin in 1956 is nothing but after-dinner talk in comparison. This detailed assault on Mao is far more violent and far-reaching. As you know, the so-called Gang of Four, which included Mao's wife, were seen to carry the can for him – for all the excesses of the Great Leap Forward and the Cultural Revolution. The appalling loss of life, millions—'

'Yep. That's all for sure, Jimmy, although at the

Gang's trial, one of them – it was even Mao's wife, I think – said, didn't she, that she had simply followed her husband's orders?'

'Exactly. That harpy Chiang Ch'ing wasn't just trying to save her neck, she was probably telling the truth for once – complete with tears! All right ... This faction – from Politburo and Military – wanted to use the formal indictment of Mao in parallel with the Gang's trial. However, you can imagine, a lot of other top brass couldn't stomach the idea, didn't want to know about it. But the *main* objection – dead right – was that an attack on Mao himself would divide China and set the country alight. So, the indictment was held back.'

'Party splits and so on isn't exactly news to us, is it? I've seen Agency estimates—'

'Us!' Ma cut the American off with one word. 'It's not us who count! If that paper is now published in the West, there's no way it can be kept from the Chinese public at large. For two generations Mao was God to eight hundred million people ... It will create chaos, anarchy. There at least *we*, back home, are in agreement with Peking thinking.' Jimmy Ma was pounding away at his knee again. 'Apart from a leadership split, the country itself will be torn apart – the people couldn't take it.'

'That's an extreme view, Jimmy. Anyway, go on – I'm listening carefully.'

'The Russians will get involved in a big way – whatever your analysts are saying about economic difficulties. Brezhnev may be smiling and signing treaties in the West – fine, but *you,* you're not his real competition. *That* is the old guard in Peking. The Soviets still want only one revolutionary centre in the world – *Moscow.* And then there are all the long-standing territorial claims ... With chaos in China, they'll support anything that's rocking the present regime there. In that turmoil, not least there are the Uighur separatists in Sinkiang who will act with a vengeance – and the Soviets will certainly leap on *that* bandwagon. And you know well that they've been supporting and stirring up the

Uighurs for years. For God's sake, Lou, they've still got twenty divisions on the Sinkiang border with China!'

'No way Washington will buy this without—'

'To hell with Washington – they don't know half of it!' Jimmy Ma was leaning forward, his fists clenched and his body tensed with urgency. 'Get this: our own forces are on preparatory alert since Tuesday. You may not be advised here, but your Headquarters will have picked it from Sigint, even if they don't know what to make of it. They're on a roll, Lou, they're getting set.'

Appleton sat quite still, absorbed in a struggle to fight off the easy option of disbelief. His teeth clamped the pipe in a corner of his mouth and his eyes were fixed on Jimmy Ma with grim attention.

'Along with a few others, I'm a dissenting voice; otherwise I wouldn't be here,' the Chinese continued, 'but by and large, the Military Command believes the moment we've been waiting for – for a generation – will arrive very soon after that document is published. We thought we could control it – once it was in our possession ... use it when and how we wanted. But we don't *have* the goddamn thing!'

Ma got up and leaned against the front of the desk.

'Are you following me, Lou?'

'Yes,' replied Appleton tersely.

'Okay. A lot of people, westerners included, expected a new look in Taiwan a couple of years ago when our President Chiang Kai-shek died, even if the dynasty continues with the son. In fact, little has changed. The thinking among important groups in the Military is the same as ever, and that's where the real KMT* power is. And they – me, too, if you like – are riding high on the economic boom, like the rest. Taiwan streets are lined with fancy computers and high-class sneakers, but the stuff is piled so high nobody sees the slogans any more. It's *always* been dismissed in the West, of course, but the priority is still the

---

* KMT – Chinese Nationalist party on Taiwan, often used for the Republic of China.

same as ever: regaining control of the Mainland when the time comes. You don't believe it?'

'I hear what you're saying.' Appleton smiled thinly

'The military have the ear of the President – they're talking about "the right moment" and persuading him that he's going to make history.'

Appleton stabbed the chewed-up pipe-stem at Jimmy Ma and shook his stubble-head.

'Look, Jimmy, we both know that Taiwan just doesn't have the firepower or backup to launch an invasion of mainland China. It's all largely defensive – okay, effective, but defensive, even supposing some upheaval over there – goddamnit!'

A wary smile appeared on his face, but it didn't last long. The visitor had something else to say.

'What you're really waiting to hear is this: the Deputy Chief of the Supreme Command accompanied by General Li, our top Air Force man and two or three other senior officers went to Moscow last Saturday. And that's something you, the Agency – *nobody* – knows. Would you like to have a large bet on it?'

'Good God,' murmured Appleton, 'I don't like the sound of that at all.' The gleam from the silver cap of his pen showed that he was writing again. He then slapped his hands on the glass-topped desk and stood up. He towered over the Chinese.

'This is going to create one helluva furore in Washington,' he said.

'If that document gets published, it's going to be more than a furore! And with the Soviets... I don't see how you could stay out of it.' Ma eased himself back into his chair again. 'In short, forget the Gulf or the Middle East – China will be the stage for the next big war, and it's going to happen very quickly.'

Appleton pushed at two buttons on the desk intercom. 'Tell me, Jimmy, in what sense are you a dissenting voice?'

'I'm as much committed to the recovery of the mainland as the rest – but not like this. The risk is too great, the

eleven

NEVER IN HIS LIFE had Larry Fenton been so thrown out of gear. The shock of Harper's death drew with it a fast-rising tide of fear that really had never been far away. He felt dazed and battered, like a boxer stepping out of the ring after a surprise loss. He left the *Review* building and walked into the heat and clamour of the late morning in Hong Kong Central.

One thought was paramount in Fenton's mind: at the *Review,* he had been listening to news of his own murder: it was clear that Jack Harper had indeed been mistaken for him. If the general physical likeness and dress had not already been enough, the Australian had, with tragic clowning, added a refinement in borrowing Fenton's hat.

Fear brought not only the common unpleasant physiological symptoms; it also quickly bred in Fenton a certain anger at having a generally well-ordered life disturbed. And the anger was attended by a grim stubbornness to continue as if there had been no upset.

His reactions became uncharacteristically abrupt, brutal even. Walking back to the Foreign Correspondents Club, twice he was involved in small incidents in the street. On the cluttered pavement, a Chinese man, poorly dressed, but not in rags, accosted him with the affected cringing, half-bent style of a beggar. Fenton would normally have ignored the man, but he brusquely swept a heavy flailing 'get-out-of-my-way' blow ahead of him. It was not a fighting blow – Fenton was not a fighting man – but it had a lot of weight behind it. The Chinese was pushed off balance and fell over. A few people stopped to stare. Fenton hurried on without looking back.

Then, near the Club, something else happened. He was halfway over a pedestrian crossing on the busy street when a small motorbike with a pillion rider took off suddenly and scraped by Fenton. Something caught in the jacket over his arm. He spun round violently, and swung another arching blow that barely missed the back of the pillion rider. The coat tore free, and the bike roared away. Again a few curious people stopped briefly to stare at him. He slipped on the coat, and in another minute he had arrived at the Club.

A dozen or so journalists were idling around, but nobody seemed to be particularly interested in his arrival. He ordered a beer and took it with him to one of the telephones in the bureau area.

'There have been several calls for you, Mr Fenton.' It was the operator at the Golden Park hotel. 'Maybe two are urgent.'

'Yes, I'll look after that this evening when I come back.'

A grimace of defiance flashed across his face. Of course he wouldn't be going near the place.

'Put me through to the bar, please. I want to leave a message.'

The earpiece clicked, paused, buzzed, revealed a fragment of somebody else's conversation and then buzzed again. It was the usual less than perfect switchboard.

'Charlie?'

'Ah, Mr Fennen sir! You wanna Black Label sent up, right?'

Fenton smiled, despite everything. He even relaxed for a second.

'No, Charlie, I'm at the ... I'm downtown. I wanted to know if by chance you had found the name of a translation—'

'I got it, sir – the client came around. American. I ask him. He works for a big American chemical company, Fidor. This lady, not agency, does a lot of work for him. She's good, recommending, sir. She fast, reliable.'

'Okay, thanks a lot, Charlie. Where do I find her?'

'One minute ... I got noted her address ...'

Fenton pulled a small note pad from his pocket as he waited. He cursed at finding the pages limp with sweat.

Small sounds of Charlie dealing with somebody at the bar came through the earpiece. But he liked the idea of an individual rather than an agency – some persuasion, buying off might well be required.

'Lady's name is Nathalie Lusen, Flat 3b, Gordon Heights. It's a block behind Causeway Bay.'

'Lusen – what nationality is that?' asked Fenton.

Charlie hesitated. 'Don't know. But must be half Chinese. She speaking other languages also, not only English.'

'Telephone number?'

'No. I don't know. Maybe in the book – I go check.'

'Never mind, Charlie, I'll do that. Thanks for your help.'

'I have the bottle ready when you come tonight, sir. You don't tell nobody and I give you one or two off account ...'

'Thanks Charlie. I'll see you later.'

It occurred to Fenton only later that barman Charlie was in a remarkably helpful, cheerful frame of mind on the telephone, which contrasted with the state of morose fatigue in which Fenton had left him late the previous day. Even if he had thought about it at the time, it would not have changed much.

*

The chance angle of a pane of glass in the Club reflected a man in bad repair. Fenton looked at himself with some discomfort, and fingered the now grubby collar and cuffs of his shirt. The air-conditioning chilled the small of his back and his chest where the sweat-soaked material had stuck to the skin. A mundane reality intruded urgently on his planning: he needed a change of clothes.

Having forsaken the convenience of a holiday hotel in pursuit of news and glory, Fenton now had no real choice but to go out and buy some essential items. However, before he went shopping, there was something else he had to do.

He borrowed a pair of scissors from the office, which

provided him also with an envelope and stamp. In a quiet corner of the Club, he carefully snipped off a second negative from one of the strips of film and folded a sheet of paper around it. He slid the small, flat packet into his right shoe. The rest of the film he put into the envelope, which he addressed to himself '*poste restante*, General Post Office, Hong Kong'. He even took care not to be observed while passing the internal mail box near the Club office.

Nobody pounced on him during the five minutes it took for him to find a men's outfitters further down the street. It was a modern, plush concern with as much imported material as that of local manufacture. In the centre of the city especially, the shop gave ample proof that Hong Kong was no longer the place to become the cheapest best-dressed man – as Fenton found, when faced with a bill of almost US $150 for two shirts, underpants and socks.

He had been the sole client at first. As he was signing away more of his dwindling wad of travellers cheques, a shadow fell across the counter. Fenton didn't look round, but he became aware of somebody standing close to him.

His chest began pounding horribly. He had to struggle to keep his eyes focussed on what he was doing. His usual signing and dating style became more meticulous than ever.

'Mr Fenton?'

The delivery was slow and deliberate from a low-pitched voice. A flash of panic made Fenton's nostrils flare, but still he managed not to look up immediately. With great precision he finished with the third cheque.

'You want my passport?' His breath bumped in his throat as he flicked his eyes up inquiringly at the shop assistant.

'That's all right, sir – thank you.'

Two heavy, spatulate fingers pushed a name card along the glass-topped counter that protected a selection of Yves Saint-Laurent ties and other Parisian rip-off items of male décor – cufflinks, collar studs and the like. '*Julius B. Bowles, US Consulate General, Hong Kong*', read the card.

'No problem. We just thought you might like a little

administrative help.'

It was American with a deep thread of some difficult to place accent – the sort of calm, academic and wise-sounding noise that Henry Kissinger used to make at his most deceptive.

Fenton tried not to let it show, but it was with a huge surge of relief that he turned to look at Julius B. Bowles.

He was a short man with plump features. Some dark, wavy hair remained on a balding head, and heavy glasses emphasised a pale, indoors complexion. Properly dressed in a surprising misty-blue suit and crisp tie – which looked just as good as anything in the shop – he could have been a moneylender or anybody's lively uncle.

Screwed up with fear a moment ago, Fenton now unwound.

'You can help with the tab, if you like – $148.50.'

He didn't smile, and it sounded assured, almost aggressive. The assistant waited patiently.

Bowles chuckled immediately. He seemed not to reflect at all, and the answer wasn't quite as Fenton had expected.

'No, you go ahead, Mr Fenton, but I hope we are now going off to a good lunch – at my invitation, of course.'

Bowles was scratching the tip of his nose with a crooked forefinger; the rolled fist, half hiding his mouth, gave a hint of conspiracy to the small smile behind.

Fenton released the cheques and turned his full attention to the American. He had already made up his mind. The assistant handed him some small change and a glossy packet so smart that it helped justify the shop's high prices.

'I'm not going anywhere with you, Mr Bowles – but thanks for the offer,' said Fenton. The tone was measured, agreeable even. Fenton smiled briefly. He tucked the rustling bag under his arm; he preferred to carry it that way rather than by the two handle loops of quarter inch silk cord. He abhorred the idea of being seen with packets that proclaimed idle expense.

Bowles didn't move. He was studying Fenton intently. Because of a difference in the strength of the lenses, the unblinking left eye seemed larger than the right. His hands were tucked way behind his back. He was a debater.

'In fact, I was going to make you another sort of offer – something ... something more substantial. But you won't change your mind about lunch?'

'No thanks.'

'How much do you expect to earn from publication?' Bowles dropped his head and peered at Fenton even more closely. His heavy chin fell on his tie.

'*What* publication? And how did you manage to jump on me here – here, in this shop?' Fenton put more surprise into his voice than he really felt.

With a broad smile acknowledging a received compliment, Bowles clapped his hands softly in front of him and raised his ill-assorted eyes to the ceiling. It was a gesture that indicated that it was of course perfectly normal for the US Consulate General to know exactly what Fenton was about at all times.

Bowles turned to the shop assistant who was repacking some other items shown to Fenton. He cracked out a few words in Cantonese and beckoned to Fenton to join him at a low table and easy chairs set in a corner of the boutique. This courtesy convenience for customers made Fenton think of the prices again.

'He's bringing a couple of beers – you look as if you could use one.' Bowles stared at Fenton's dirty, sweat-darkened shirt.

Fenton was aware that the American had taken charge, smoothly and without too much push. He also calculated that if he didn't want to be seen around town with a US official, he was already compromised – within the confines of the shop – by the encounter. He sat down. The assistant arrived at once with two opened bottles of San Miguel covered by upturned glasses. It was a free service provided by many Hong Kong shops, often without the asking.

'Well, how much could you expect to earn from an article, or even several, based on that material?' Bowles had ignored Fenton's first disclaimer.

'No idea.' It was a brusque reply, but Fenton was fascinated to know where it would lead. Bowles had poured out a glass of beer and pushed it across the table.

'Supposing,' he said slowly in his deep, thickly reassuring voice, 'suppose a couple of thousand dollars ...? Maybe more ...' His eyes never left Fenton's face. 'We could, say, double that easily.' He sank back heavily in the chair and sipped at the beer, watching and waiting.

Fenton stared back. He felt a sudden, deadening disappointment. The magic carpet had slipped away from under him. Could that really be all there was to it?

'You see, it's an interesting story,' Bowles was saying, 'but something the US and allied governments would like to see handled in a particular way, as you will appreciate.'

The events flashed through Fenton's mind yet again: the thugs dragging away the Chinese from the hotel, people searching his room, following him all over the town, the murder of Jack Harper – surely all that suggested that the material, the story or whatever it was, was worth a lot more than the few thousand dollars that the Americans seemed to be offering. And he also had his own gut feeling about what was at stake.

Then, suddenly, he could read the answer in Bowles' face, in his whole manner and approach. He didn't *know* what was going on! It was simply a try-on to see if whatever it was could be bought out of the market cheaply – as a precaution, in case it was something explosive. Bowles had some information, that was clear, but not nearly enough. Fenton released a one-syllable laugh, a snap of scorn.

'Yes, well, Mr Bowles, as you too will appreciate; I am going to handle this in my own way – as a journalist.'

He stood up to leave. The other man was writing something on a slip of paper.

'You're British – I've used the pounds sign,' he said with a slight smile.

Fenton glanced at the paper on which was scribbled a small addition sum composed of three double figures with the correct total under the line. The sterling sign suggested the sort of jottings people do on cheque stubs.

'If you change your mind, read the figures down. The total is irrelevant. You can reach me on that private number or leave a message. It wouldn't necessarily be our last offer, of course.'

Fenton thrust the paper into the top pocket of his jacket.

'Thank you for the beer,' he said. He hadn't realised that it was free. He nodded farewell and walked quickly out of the shop.

Julius B. Bowles, as he would have it, remained seated and nursing his glass while watching the prey slip away. But it wouldn't be for long, he thought.

twelve

'YOU DIDN'T SAY you were coming over straight away!'
Only half of the young woman's face was visible from the six-inch gap that the security chain allowed in the barely opened door. It was enough for Fenton to recognise the sort of svelte beauty that he was sometimes given to chasing in his dreams.

'Yes, I'm sorry – but it's quite urgent.'

He glanced, up and down, at the rest of what the gap had to offer. He noted a tanned, well-kept foot in an open sandal and then a long stretch of some silky white material belonging to one of those light, close-cut trouser suits which, on the right body, look stunning. Back to the face, Fenton saw features that suggested Asia, but there was something in the *regard*, a particular aura, that looked as if it had grown up in the West.

'And you're a friend of Clark's?'

'Well, as I told you on the phone, the company, Fidor, recommended me to come to you.'

Fenton was pushing his luck, he knew. It wasn't strictly true about the recommendation; it had merely been barman Charlie's idea.

One dark brown eye studied Fenton for an instant longer. Then the loose chain splattered against the wood and the door opened fully.

'Come on in, then, and we'll see what it's about.'

Nathalie Lusen closed the door and replaced the chain. She led the way from the entrance hall. Preoccupied as he was, the girl's beauty in her simple but chic outfit stunned him. Late twenties, Fenton thought, or perhaps a little more. Slim, and taller than most women in this part of the world, she had an easy, balanced walk without it being deformed into the prancing gait of a fashion model.

As he followed her into what was evidently the workroom, a trace of perfume in the air reminded Fenton that he was in bad order. Had it not been for wanting to get away quickly from Bowles, he would have changed into his new clothes back at the shop. He felt embarrassed, and this only increased his sweating, although the apartment seemed cool after the clammy heat of the street.

As the girl pushed a chair towards him, the telephone on the desk rang. She nodded excuses to Fenton and picked up the receiver. She was speaking Mandarin. Unlike many of the female voices Fenton had heard in the last few days, there was nothing shrill or piping about it; it was a soft, low, almost musical noise, with whispered sibilants and purrs. He'd never heard anything like it in his life. He looked around the room.

The long desk, heaped with papers, was not unlike his own back in Rome, with its accumulation of the usual office clutter. A second typewriter and a Xerox copying machine to one side added to the 'commercial' touch. It occurred to Fenton that the three-tiered bookshelf on wheels – like a converted meal trolley – was an idea to be borne in mind. The one here contained an impressive array of dictionaries in several languages along with a mass of other reference books.

Fenton smiled a little at recognising a series of mildly titillating Aubrey Beardsley pen-and-ink reproductions hung on the wall behind the desk. Another wall was partly fabric-covered in a haphazard way by cheap prints of oriental boudoir and battle scenes. These were the only decorations, and apart from the desk working area, the place had a 'spare room', untidy or 'just-moved-in' feel about it. Two disconnected table lamps were parked on the floor next to a large laundry basket propped against a huge stack of magazines and other paper.

Still on the phone, the girl turned and smiled at him, and flapped a slim, well-manicured hand in an apologetic gesture.

Fenton pulled on his jacket in an effort to be more

presentable. At one point, the girl faced him squarely with a look of frank curiosity. Then she gave a quick smile and turned away again. It was mostly a conversation illustrated with a string of facial expressions and gestures indicating mild impatience or boredom with what the person on the other end was saying. The receiver was finally clapped down.

'Sorry about that. Well, Mr Fenton – that's right, isn't it – what is it you want me to translate?'

Instantly Fenton was reminded that the negative strip was still packed into his shoe. God, what an absurd little hassle! He felt a renewed outbreak of sweating on his face.

'Yes ... I ... Look, forgive me, but I wonder ... Before we start, could I first use your bathroom?'

'It's through here.' Nathalie Lusen pushed herself off the edge of the desk on which she had perched in a pose that Fenton, despite his disarray, had found elegant and titillating. He grabbed his parcel of new clothes, and followed the girl.

They passed through the adjoining room. The bed and various cupboards had an uncomplicated – utility even – look about them, and the general décor was plain and lacking in frills for the sort of bedroom Fenton would have associated with a woman of Nathalie Lusen's style.

'There we are ...' The tone was matter of fact. She switched some long, dark strands of hair from one shoulder to the other. 'My guess is that you want to get cleaned up. Use the shower – anything. You won't be charged extra.' She said with a smile. 'But you'll have to pay time and a half if I have to drop any current work to do yours quickly.'

'Back in five minutes – and thanks,' said Fenton. He closed the door.

As he undressed, he could hear in the distance the encouraging clatter of a typewriter being used at professional speed.

*

'It will need tidying up later. But that's it – a first draft finished.'

Nathalie Lusen was scanning through another sheet and pencilling in small corrections. There were four pages of close typing in English for only one of the fine-print pages of the original Chinese.

With a family slide viewer, normally hand-held, the practical aspect had been tricky. By rigging it up with a more powerful light source from one of the table lamps, and using a system of two magnifying glasses, she was just able to read the Chinese script.

The exercise had taken almost four hours, and it was now early evening. It had not been continuous work; the laboriousness of the task was relieved by several short breaks. They had begun to talk easily and Fenton found himself being drawn into an almost conspiratorial dialogue with the charming and efficient Nathalie.

'That's fine,' said Fenton, 'enough for today.'

'I don't follow politics closely. Not my line. But I must say this looks a bit out of the ordinary. And you still haven't told me where it comes from.'

Again an open, flashing smile put Fenton to the test. He wasn't far from reacting, but prudence prevailed. He retrieved the negative strip and slipped it into his wallet with the care given to handling a priceless postage stamp.

'It was hard on the eyes,' Nathalie continued, 'but frankly I'm quite glad you dropped by. Your stuff is more interesting than an ad blurb I'm working on – a wonder drug for piles, of all things ...' Another small smile, and then 'I can probably borrow a proper projector tomorrow. It will make things a lot easier.'

A flicker of disappointment intruded on Fenton's now buoyant mood. He had expected something more than the word 'interesting', even though it was based on only a fragment of the whole document. He gathered the papers together in a pile on the desk.

'You don't sound very surprised,' he said, hoping to elicit a more robust comment.

'Oh, but I am. I've never read anything like it. You can see ...' A delicate hand opened like a fan pointing towards the papers: 'It's a verbal assassination – in a kind of legal language – of some senior Party leader. If all that Gang of Four business was still going on, I would have said it was aimed at one of them. Perhaps they're setting up number five! The name doesn't actually appear in this extract, but it will be in the rest. I can't *imagine* that it's Mao himself – if it was, they'd all be on course for civil war over there!'

Politics may not have been Nathalie Lusen's line, thought Fenton, but she could evidently string a few thoughts together.

'I could have a quick look through now, if you like, and we could—'

'Tomorrow,' said Fenton decisively.

'Well, must say I'm a bit tired. It's not easy, concentrating on all that Party jargon ...'

She stopped and stared into space. For moments, she seemed to be a long way from Hong Kong. Then a quick little movement of her head seemed to shake off some memories.

'Let's have a drink. You take whisky, Larry?' Another sudden, marvellous smile.

Fenton was not quite undone, but during the course of the long afternoon he had been gradually unwinding – or perhaps unwound. He was enthralled by this attractive young woman who, even if her origins were mixed – Russian father, Chinese mother, she had said – more than fulfilled his most extravagant and long-standing fantasies about the ideal Asian female.

*

Fenton felt more upbeat than at any time since arriving in Hong Kong. He was excited by the obvious news value of the text and more than happy with the quality of Nathalie's work. The flow of 'after-work' conversation, eased on by a few more drinks, relaxed him further. And he found himself calling on long dormant resources of charm.

These seemed to be having an effect, as Nathalie responded with encouraging warmth. With a small shot of rapture in his veins, Fenton inwardly celebrated the fact that not only had he hired a translator, but also that the scene looked set for a close-quarter encounter of another kind. Encouraging atmosphere there certainly was, but Fenton felt that he was probably too exhausted, drained, for making further advance then and there, and his mind settled more for a delicious prospect in reserve.

They were still installed on either side of the desk. In fact, there were no easy chairs in the room. Nathalie refilled both of their glasses. Fenton was not used to women drinking whisky, and Nathalie had seemed to want to keep pace with him. But this time she left her glass untouched. She stood up.

'Stay put and finish your drink, Larry. I'm going to get us something to eat.' Nathalie went through to a small kitchen area leading off the main room. Fenton was left with his whisky and to ponder his luck. A few minutes later, Nathalie called out:

'So, "tourist from Rome" ... where are you staying?'

The comfort, the element of excitement and sense of relief suddenly faded. Fenton remembered that he was a hunted man.

'I'll sort that out later,' he said. 'I mean, I think I'll be changing hotels.'

'You seem a nice enough guy, Larry, but I get the impression that you're on the run from something ... or someone.'

Nathalie came back, fussed around, tidying up the desk, but she was looking at Fenton all the time, inviting an explanation. There was none. His mind was juggling with all sorts of 'going-to-ground' theories. But how did people do it in an unfamiliar country? Perhaps the Club could help, or if he went back to the *Review* they might ...

'I don't mind a bit of intrigue from time to time,' Nathalie was saying, 'I mean, I wouldn't harbour criminals

– but I don't think you're that!'

Again there was that brief, fabulous smile.

'You can stay here, if you want.' She waved a sheaf of papers at a divan against a wall, and on which was piled office clutter – old calendars, magazines, folders and the like.

'It opens out into a bed,' Nathalie added.

*

Fenton managed not to tell everything. The temptation had been there – over a simple meal of fried rice and thin beef strips cooked with black mushrooms and that thick, spicy sauce that only the Chinese seem able to make.

What Fenton talked of freely, because Nathalie had the charm anyway to seem interested, concerned his life back in Rome and his cheerfully acid views on the state of the Italian nation in general. The evening – two or three hours – passed easily and then, quite suddenly, Fenton stood up and gave a washed-out smile of apology.

'It's been a long day, Nathalie. Thank you again, for all your help and ... hospitality, but I do need to turn in.'

He used the bathroom and came back to find that Nathalie had organised the divan, which she presented with fluttering hands, as if doing a magician's number. It had indeed unfolded into a stark but already sheet-laid bed. Fenton smiled his thanks, sat down and started to undress. Nathalie hovered around discreetly, making small arrangements, hanging up his clothes by the divan, and then left him to it.

Stripped to his underpants, Fenton stayed sitting on the edge of the couch for a few minutes longer. He stroked his eyebrows, and pinched the bridge of his nose, as he tried to work out a course of action for the next day or two. Ideas came and went but without real coherence. Planning was anyway confused by thoughts on the dazzling Nathalie. His eyelids were dropping.

He got up, switched off the office lights and then settled

down in his allotted place. Sheer tiredness and a lot of alcohol made the thing seem far more comfortable than it really was. He lay there for some minutes, lost in his thoughts. Nathalie's bedroom door was slightly open. The soft light from a low wattage lamp was on. Fenton was dimly aware of flickering shadows that danced insistently on the floor just outside the door. Some radio or cassette music played softly. Suddenly his heavy eyes were wide open. Twice he had a glimpse of the girl, gloriously naked, apparently hanging up or putting away clothes.

Fenton's mind raced. No woman, in such a situation, leaves her bedroom door open and trips around without a stitch on and then—

'Nathalie ...' Fenton heaved himself off the couch. He walked across and tapped on the door.

'Come on in, Larry – you don't have to mess around out there. That is, unless ...'

Fenton found that the dubious dictum of the sports coach, 'fatigue is only a state of mind' had something in it, after all.

*

He had still not adjusted to the time difference. After only a couple of hours of sleep, he was wide awake at 3.45 a.m. The girl at his side, facing him and breathing lightly, clearly had no such problems. A cheap bedside lamp was still on. Nathalie's face was smooth and serene. Her long dark hair, nicely dishevelled only an hour or two ago, was now back in fashion-plate order. Traces of rose-pink lipstick, however, had stayed smudged on one cheek. It all had the look of a contented woman sleeping luxuriously. The image, the presence, provoked a quick flutter of excitement in Fenton and immediately he was brought to the brink again. But he hesitated, concerned that he might wreck it all.

He looked around idly. The bedroom door was still open. Outside in the office, a small red glow at table level caught his attention. It was a sort of signal light that announces that a piece of electrical apparatus is on standby. Fenton was mildly curious. He slipped carefully out of bed and edged his way into the office area.

It was the Xerox copier. Fenton stared at it for some seconds. He looked down, and in a nearby waste bin he saw a screwed-up piece of paper.

Under the faint light, Fenton spread out the sheet. The top two-thirds were blank. However, at the lower edge of the page, traces of typing were just visible. Wallowing in pleasurable thoughts and marvelling at his luck a moment earlier, he was now seized by a sudden, cold dread. Enough of the translation had stuck in his head for him to know what he was looking at.

It was an unsuccessful photocopy. The girl had evidently not noticed that something had appeared on the sheet. No doubt other correct copies had been made of the four pages of translation that were still neatly stacked on the desk. She could have done it while he was in the bathroom or, more likely, while he was asleep.

Fenton raged at himself for being so stupid, for being taken in. Of course it was too good to be true! How could a girl like Nathalie Lusen welcome into her apartment – and bed – a total stranger of the likes of Larry Fenton!

He was furious, as much with himself as with Nathalie. He fought off a momentary urge to haul the girl from the sheets and physically force her to destroy the copies she had certainly made. Then a whole lot of questions crowded into his mind. The anger gave way to fear, once more, that seemed to return like bouts of fever. But Fenton was also driven by obstinacy, a determination not to be beaten.

Bitch! Was it the Chinese? The British? The Americans – the CIA? Whoever it was, the scenario had been irresistible. Alarmed, but mainly enraged, Fenton knew he had to run – and now! He first bundled up his clothes – which had been so nicely hung – then he retrieved the translation paper from the desk. He glanced beyond the door at the bed. Nathalie had not stirred.

In a sort of last, overall little gesture of defiance, with a grim smile he unplugged the telephone: 'Might help a bit...' he thought. He then eased himself out of flat 3b at Gordon Heights. Once in the lobby, deserted at 4 a.m., he threw on his clothes. As he walked away, his mind was fixed on the conviction that the girl had not acted purely on her own account.

*

'Mr Fenton!'

Even before he heard the voice and the hurrying footsteps behind him, he sensed that somebody was there. In fact, Fenton was looking down the street at a solitary car that was reversing quickly back in his direction.

'Hey there, Mr Fenton!'

He wheeled round. A European of average build was half running towards him. Fenton turned again to look at the car, which had stopped in front of him. One man got out.

Fenton felt confusion and fear, and the instinct to run almost had its way. But he stayed still. After all, the way 'Mr Fenton' was called out didn't sound hostile.

He never saw it coming. The blow was precise and efficient. He felt a violent thud in the head and a flash of intense nausea. As his eyes rolled round, they recorded one last fleeting image. It was somebody else bounding out of a doorway up the road and charging towards him. Fenton recognised the round body and short legs of Julius B. Bowles moving at surprising speed.

thirteen

FENTON CAME ROUND in phases, with patchy recognition of what was happening. At one stage there was a battery of Chinese faces peering down at him. He knew that he was enclosed, confined in some way. Confused images of glass, polished metal, levers and gauges made an image of an operating theatre or some terrifyingly refined torture chamber. Another blurred vision was of mutilated animals hung up around him in a kind of frightful warning.

Then the Chinese were there again. One man in a gaudy Hawaiian shirt was shouting at him from a mouth of black and gold teeth. Fenton was in a sitting position. Gradually he realised what he had to do.

For some moments he couldn't find the right lever, but he finally opened the door and staggered out onto the pavement. The brightly dressed Chinese fronted up to him aggressively. With his arms wind-milling, he was shouting over and over again:

'My car! My car! You unnerstan? My car!'

Fenton looked around. He was dazed and the pain throbbed so intensely in his head that it brought on spasms of nausea without the relief of actually throwing up. He took in the adjacent shop with its rows of obscenely naked ducks hung on hooks in the company of skinned rabbits and snakes.

He felt for his wallet. It had gone. No, it hadn't. It had been replaced in the wrong inside pocket of his jacket. His money seemed to be intact. He pulled out a $20 bill and handed it to the complaining Chinese. The latter folded it away with a sudden smile that conveyed grotesque complicity.

Fenton tottered away. The small crowd dispersed and went about their early morning business. They were sniggering derisively at the drunken foreigner who obviously had emerged late from a bar or brothel and then kipped down in the car. They were also amused because the vehicle had nothing to do with the neighbourhood slick-mouth who had pocketed the $20.

Fenton glanced giddily at his watch. It was 6.30 am. He was conscious of the envelope still in his left shoe. Although he had evidently been searched, they had not found the papers or, he assumed, the negative that he had also slipped into the packet before leaving ... leaving Nathalie. God, what a woman! It came back to him and it seemed like a dream – the enchantment, the incredible facility of it all, and then the evident treachery.

Several minutes of walking made him steadier on his feet and clearer in the head. Some landmarks began to make sense to him: the harbour was where it should be, the tall buildings ahead identified Hong Kong Central and the immediate agglomeration of bars and dance halls signalled that he was in the red-light area of Wanchai. He wandered on, telling himself that that fresh air and exercise were overcoming the recurrent waves of nausea.

Half an hour later he arrived at a large compound, housing two modern five-floor office blocks. Inside the protective wire fencing all round the area were scores of assorted police vehicles. He guessed that this was the Arsenal Street Police Headquarters. The proximity of that building made Fenton think hard.

He walked into a nearby bar-café. He asked for a coffee and pointed to a doughnut-like lump of pastry on the counter. It contained something unexpectedly salty, which he couldn't eat. He settled for a cellophane-wrapped packet of biscuits instead; after a second coffee, he began to feel much better. The headache, in the general sense, had all but gone and he was left only with pain in a localised area behind his right ear. Fenton felt the area gingerly, and then looked at his fingers. There was no bleeding. 'Just a surface graze,' he muttered to himself. But how can one be hit with that amount of evident force, he wondered, without there being blood all over the place?

He left the bar and walked on. An endless line of junks and sampans nudged the waterfront and jetties. In the stretch of the harbour beyond, a huge cargo ship was creeping to its berth among the bustle of small craft. The sounds and smells were those of the start of any day in Hong Kong. Fenton turned back from the harbour's edge and made for a main road. He took another hesitating look at Police Headquarters and then cast around to find a taxi.

That strange last sight – he was sure that it had not been imagined – of Julius B. Bowles galloping towards him was one of the more insistent images in his mind. The American had evidently arrived too late to help him. But what had happened, then, to Bowles? Fenton decided to find out.

fourteen

'YES, BUT WHAT'S your business, sir?'
Wary, not quite unfriendly, the question was put by a forty-something woman secretary who had come to the reception desk at the US Consulate General.

'If it's a visa problem—'

'Just tell Mr Bowles that I would like to continue the discussion we started yesterday.' Fenton managed to keep the tone measured.

The secretary, with her flat-heeled shoes, was still as tall as the visitor; she faced him squarely with a look that conveyed both scepticism and only mild interest. Her height alone was often an immediate advantage in subduing 'difficult' visitors at reception. This one was not quite that, but he had stood his ground. Without further word, she turned and went back to the inner sanctum.

Having arrived at the Consulate at 9.15 am, Fenton spent twenty minutes in the reception area, in which some easy chairs and a vast rack of local and American reading matter was available. Waiting around was evidently expected of visitors to such places. Still, it could have been worse. As Fenton was finally led to another office, he passed a large hall that served as a marshalling area for the crowds of Hong Kong Chinese queuing for US visas.

Julius B. Bowles jerked his head back from a small peephole strategically mounted in a wall.

'I've never seen the man before.' He shrugged and walked away towards his own adjoining office. His tall secretary followed him.

'But he says you wanted to buy something, and were even offering him lunch.'

Bowles interrupted with a snort of impatience and flapped his hands.

126

'Come on, Grace, there's a stack of paper to get through! So, *please*, send the guy on his way. He's obviously a nutcase. I don't want to know about it.'

At the door, the secretary turned to Bowles again. Her face was pinched up into an expression of fretful reproach.

'He doesn't look or talk like a nut case,' Grace said firmly.

'Okay, okay.' Bowles was exasperated. 'I'll tell them on the third floor – and that's it. Now just get rid of him!'

He snatched up the internal telephone and dialled three digits.

'Joe, you'd better know that there's been an upmarket Brit character at reception called Fulton or something. He claims that he met me downtown yesterday. It's horseshit. The guy's crazy. Okay ... six foot, about forty-five, greying hair, slight stoop—'

'All right, thanks. Listen, Jubee, I don't want to sound dramatic, but I've got some real problems. Been here all night and I'm tired. We'll be in touch later.'

For the previous twenty-four hours Joe Silverman had indeed been preoccupied – and still was – with the murder of a key agent, Jack Harper, the one codenamed Feedback. In other circumstances, a visitor with a strange story in the Consular section might have attracted Silverman's casual interest. However, the Harper assassination had for the moment effaced all other business.

Silverman and his staff had gone through all the paper still available on file in Hong Kong, for any detail, any clue that would give a lead on why Harper had been killed. There was nothing. And during the night, the series of telegrams from Headquarters summarising the case had provided nothing else to work on.

He was drinking one more coffee from an automatic dispenser when an apparently unrelated message arrived from Washington with a startling priority rating. The Feedback killing was temporarily pushed aside. Another name clattered out on the machine from a deciphered telex tape. Silverman grabbed the phone and stabbed at some numbers.

'Jubee, tell me again very quietly, very accurately, who he was – that guy downstairs you were telling me about ...' The voice was tense, but the delivery was slow and deliberate. Silverman had the good policeman's instinct not to prompt.

Julius B. Bowles sighed noisily into the telephone mouthpiece. He signed two papers before replying: 'Fulton, Forton ... er ... Just a moment.'

He handed the papers to his secretary and then clapped the telephone on his thigh. 'Grace, what was that weirdie called, the one who wanted to see me?'

He got the answer immediately, but waited until the secretary had left the office before speaking again.

'I noted it all down,' he lied, 'and got a sight of him in reception. Fenton it was, Larry Fenton. English by the sound and look of him. Do you want—'

Silverman jumped up and clapped the receiver down, cutting Bowles off in mid-sentence.

'Call Marriot and tell him I'm on my way to see him urgently!' he yelled out to his secretary. Then he was running down the corridor towards a back exit from the building.

'Jesus,' he was shouting to himself, 'the guy was actually *here* in the Consulate – what an all time, mind-bending fuck-up!'

*

Larry Fenton's dismissal at the reception desk had been polite but firm. His immediate reaction was one of almost detached resignation at being sent on his way; but once outside the Consulate premises, as he walked slowly on down Garden Road, it was more stupor and outrage that took hold. And that feeling was tinged with fear. A couple of taxis passed. Fenton waved down a third.

'Downtown – Post Office, please!'

The car waited while he collected his packet from the

poste restante. The taxi then drove him straight to Kai Tak airport. There, with comforting ease, Fenton got his return-ticket destination adjusted; he felt that London rather than Rome would be the right place to launch his momentous story project.

During the couple of hours' wait for the BA flight, Larry Fenton came to a decision. It would be around 10 a.m. in Europe. With any luck, his old flame, hopefully still flickering, would be at home in London, and he knew that he could count on her. He telephoned from the airport Post Office, spent a couple of happy minutes on the call, and then mailed the precious envelope addressed to Joanna Waley at Rutland Gate, SW7.

*

There may have been a slight vibration in the room, but it was more the fast-moving shadow from the vast window area that made the two men look round.

Silverman got up and watched a huge jet touch down a quarter of a mile away down the Kai Tak landing strip. There were two salvos of bluish smoke as several kilos of rubber burnt off the undercarriage wheels.

'He must be around,' said Silverman. 'They'll be boarding any minute now.'

'It could be a deception. Sacrificing his luggage, taking another flight.'

The quiet remark came from the other man still seated in a small soundproofed room set apart from the public areas. As he spoke, he reached down and with a two-handed grasp wrenched his right leg up and over the left knee. The limb seemed to dangle limply for a moment, and then it looked normal. A heavy walking stick was propped against the chair.

'Anyway I guess he's just keeping his head down until the last moment. He's obviously frightened – with good reason. And he's been hiding for most of the time. As you know, his bags ... Hasn't even been back to the hotel.'

Marriot's face was tanned but it was noticeably lined and this, together with almost white hair, trimmed short, made him look older than his fifty years. His features, bearing and dress belonged to any of the longer-established London clubs. He was the Governor's advisor on security matters, responsible directly to London and right now he represented the British government's last word as far as the Fenton affair was concerned.

'The point is, he's running! When he comes through that door, why can't you have him detained for ... for obstructing the police? ... Failing to report a felony? ... Or some other fancy phrase that you British are so good at. There must be *something* we can pin him on!' Silverman had turned back from the window and was gently slapping his palms together in frustration.

'There's nothing valid to go on. The Governor just won't have it. It was only reluctantly that he agreed to a last-minute interview. Neither London nor H.E. will countenance anything that might provoke Chinese reaction in Hong Kong. Back in the UK we can handle it. The sooner Fenton is out of here the better. We can try persuasion – straight talk to get him to hand it over, but I doubt that it will work. If you were a journalist, Joe, what would you do with material like that?'

'It's so goddamn feeble – a crisis situation and you can't even get your priorities—'

Silverman's fulminations were abruptly broken off. The door opened and the much sought-after Fenton was ushered in by a Hong Kong Police Inspector who introduced his find with a strong Yorkshire accent. The fact that the policeman was none other than the one Fenton had tried to approach at the hotel only aggravated his mood of aggressive impotence. Fenton's face betrayed his feelings; he looked sour and tense, and ready for a fight. The police officer left immediately.

'Marriot ...' He remained seated, but was offering his hand. Fenton didn't move. With a faint flick of the eyebrows indicating resigned surprise, Marriot let his hand beckon towards the American as if that was what it had been pushed out for in the first place.

'This is a colleague from the United States Consulate.'

The American moved across to Fenton with a wide smile. He had a certain way with him.

'Joe Silverman ...' he said, and he, too, had his hand outstretched. This time Fenton gave his own hand in return, warily, as if expecting another assault. Then he noticed the gnarled and hefty stick of a disabled man hooked on the chair. In some way the item was reassuring. He relaxed a little and looked at his watch.

'Don't worry,' Marriot said, 'the aircraft is not going to leave without you. You know what this is all about. I am here in the Governor's name and in a broader sense as a representative of British Intelligence interests. It should be clear to you that Mr Silverman is—'

'Yes,' broke in Larry Fenton, 'CIA!'

Silverman winced inwardly at the name of the Agency being bandied about. He dragged up a chair.

'Let's sit down and talk it through,' he said. Fenton again glanced at his watch and then at Marriot.

'Forget the plane,' the latter said. 'Everybody else will be crammed into a bus shortly – but there's a car outside that will take you for boarding. We've also got your luggage from the hotel. It's already been checked onto the plane.'

Marriot was wearing his most reassuring smile. Fenton sighed and sat down.

'What do I say? Thank you?' The sarcasm was so heavy that both the other men stared at him, surprised. This enraged Fenton.

'My God – you've got some damn funny manners between you! You have me beaten senseless, then – so you say – collect my bags, rifled through no doubt, and now you want me to sit down and talk!'

'What the devil are you talking about – "beaten senseless"?' said Marriot sharply.

Fenton swung round in his chair, but it was to face the

American. He stabbed a finger at him.

'You know bloody well that Bowles of your outfit propositioned me yesterday and when that didn't work, your thugs clobbered me early this morning – and I can tell you that didn't work either. Bowles was there. I saw him just as I was brought down – coshed or whatever!'

Fenton had changed his mind. The reason for Bowles' refusal to meet him at the Consulate had become all too clear. Fenton had seen him running forward in the street – but it had not been to help. On the contrary, Bowles was there actually supervising the assault! So Fenton had reasoned.

The two interrogators were wide-eyed and silent. It was some seconds before Silverman reacted.

'See here, Mr Fenton, Jubee – Julius Bowles – is a Vice-Consul. He has absolutely nothing to do with us. And anyway; he says that he'd never heard of you before you arrived at the Consulate this morning.'

Fenton interrupted with a vigorous wave of his arm. He delved in his pockets. It was a clumsy operation because his hands were trembling. He fumbled with the contents, dropping an assortment of notes and bills. At last he found the name-card and the scrap of paper Bowles had given him.

'There!'

He thrust both items at Silverman in a rough moment of triumph.

'You will know, of course, how to read the numbers down for the telephone,' he added. The renewed sarcasm was smothered by the excitement in his voice.

The American studied the evidence for an instant and then handed it to Marriot.

'Ah, I know that number,' he said. 'It's the Lusen apartment out at Gordon Heights.'

'Exactly,' Fenton cried. 'And don't imagine I fell for all that. What a setup!'

Again there was a short silence. Marriot put it together first.

'Tell me, Mr Fenton, what did your Bowles look like?'

The question was quietly put. Fenton stared. Albeit with an edge of exasperation, his reply was studiedly controlled.

'About fifty, medium-short, tubby figure, sallow-looking ... er ... glasses, balding dark hair—'

'Speaking a sort of guttural but good American and wearing a bright suit?' interrupted Marriot.

'What the hell is "guttural but good American"?' Silverman muttered.

'Yes,' said Fenton. He found his mood quietening.

'God, what a nerve!' Marriot exclaimed. There was an element of shocked respect in his voice. He turned to Silverman with a wry smile.

'We know who that is ... It has to be ... friend Karpov, Alexander Karpov, our Soviet resident.'*

'That's it,' he said slowly, 'Yeh ... you're right.'

He was suddenly beaming at the equally happy Marriot. It was a moment of professional celebration from which, of course, Fenton was excluded.

Silverman stared, open-mouthed for a second.

'But how can they have zoned in so quickly?'

'Quite so.' Marriot nodded and then his eyebrows shot up. 'Wait a minute,' he said, turning his attention back to Fenton, 'you were at the Golden Park Hotel, and you went to the bar there?'

'Look,' said Fenton irritated again. 'Nathalie Lusen was recommended to me by an American concern—'

'But you went to the bar there,' Marriot persisted.

'Yes, but you're not telling me that barman Charlie is a Russian spy!'

Even as he snapped it out, Fenton wished the remark had not been so larded with ridicule.

'It's not his fault,' said Marriot, unruffled, 'he thinks he's talking to American Intelligence. Karpov hangs around there claiming to represent an American chemical company,

---

* 'Resident' – term used loosely in the trade for a Soviet agent operating under non-official cover in a foreign country.

Fidor. He works quite a lot of Japanese visitors like that –
and some American ones when he gets the chance. Yes,
well … Nathalie Lusen ... Yes, young Nathalie is a
marvellously attractive and talented handful. If you've come
across her in your travels, Mr Fenton, you have something
to write home about.'

Marriot's faint smile faded quickly.

'Yes, she's half Russian. She has problems. They got to
her a long time ago. You were "set up" all right, as you put
it – not by us, but by the KGB.'

Fenton was so dumbfounded that he didn't even hear
Silverman putting another question to him. And he had his
own point to make:

'So you knowingly leave Soviet spies running loose?
Why, in God's name, don't you arrest them – get rid of
them? It's unbelievable.'

Again it was Marriot who replied. He had one of those
old-style, well-honed BBC voices that tend to be smooth
and reassuring without quite being slick. It worked well
with a lot of the excitable people he met.

'All in good time. Those two are watched. They are
useful to us for—'

'It wasn't you who got clouted on the head this
morning,' Fenton said acidly.

'Yes, I know, I know.' For a moment Marriot looked
concerned, and there was a hint of sympathy in his voice.
Then the tone changed and became businesslike once again.

'Now, for the record, I am asking you formally to hand
over the film. You will be compensated properly. It's
potentially disastrous ...' His voice trailed off as Fenton
stood up abruptly.

'I no longer have it! And I say this to you: "potentially
disastrous" – Governments make disasters, not
newspapers!'

'You could be prosecuted under the Official Secrets
Act.'

'Balls!'

*

Marriot and Silverman stood behind a dull glass panel, watching the passengers file through the last boarding corridor to the bus. Fenton was there, having rushed off to join everybody else, rather than take the offered special treatment car.

Both the observers had passenger manifests in hand, and they were jotting down occasional notes. Then a European member of the ground staff walked back along the passage and swept his hands apart to signal that it was all over.

'What have we got, then?' Silverman asked. They were walking towards an unremarkable Ford Granada parked in the restricted zone of the airport. 'Reckon I guessed right on your own guy!' he added, with a grin. 'Small moustache, no carry-on except Duty Free plastic bag ... But I thought you said there were two?'

'One is a woman.'

'Ah ...'

'Well now,' Marriot paused and pencilled down the list of passengers. 'Uncle Lam is aboard – S.T. Lin. Here he is,' he said, showing his list to Silverman. 'So the KMT are present. And there was another man, something of a brute; I can't put a name to it, but he was definitely with Lam.'

'Yep, I got Lam, too. The other one I missed. As for the Russians, I'm real sure the supposed Austrian, Weichberger, is 100% Slav, and passenger ...' he searched down the column '... here we go – Constantin. He's anyway travelling on a Soviet official passport. And I vaguely recognise the face.'

'Right, said Marriot, 'and I think I saw yet another Russian, but I can't find a name that fits immediately.'

They reached the car. Silverman looked back for a moment. The jet had left a long, trailing smudge of smoke curving into the sky.

'Lovely party. We know that the Chinese Nationalists are aboard – and the Russians. But I couldn't see anything that looked like Peking.'

He held open the door of the Ford for his one-legged colleague.

'No ...' said Marriot slowly. He perched on the back seat, with one foot still dangling on the ground outside. He looked up at the American.

'There's a funny thing. We haven't got a scrap of hard evidence against him – a mere hint or a whisper over the years. Nothing really. But how extraordinary that he, too, should have been on that particular London flight.'

'Who's that?'

Marriot heaved his artificial leg into the car. Silverman closed the door and walked round to get in the other side, tapping the American chauffeur on the shoulder as he went.

'Well, who are you talking about?'

'G.T. Tan – Gerry Tan. He's a partner in Peeble Hunt. Suave but likeable man. UK-educated. He's a member of the Club ...'

fifteen

'THANK YOU, sir.'

The woman immigration officer at Heathrow snapped the passport closed and handed it back. There was even a bright 7.30 a.m. smile for which an exhausted and uptight Larry Fenton was grateful.

He walked quickly through to the baggage collection area where half a dozen other passengers were already hanging around the carousels.

The overhead display flashed up the belt number for Fenton's flight. He wandered slowly towards carousel indicated, with his eye roving over the scattering of people in the hall. None seemed particularly interested in him.

Then, with a small shock of fascinated recognition, he saw that his own cases, closely followed by his typewriter, were the very first things to be disgorged onto the belt. He moved forward a few steps, but then stopped. Something told him to leave the bags where they were. They had been put aboard and now taken off the plane all too easily. He would telephone British Airways later.

Of course the thought of being under surveillance had been with Fenton constantly during the long flight. The term 'nervous exhaustion' was a vague term for him and he had not experienced it before. Now he knew exactly what it meant.

A Customs officer gave him a sharp glance when he arrived at the checkpoint with no luggage at all – 'being sent on tomorrow' – but he was waved on with no questions asked.

Once through that last control, a shot of almost gleeful confidence put some spring into Fenton's step. He knew that he was the first one out. As he reached the taxi rank, a last look round told him that he was well clear of any immediate followers.

137

*

In a convoy of traffic, the taxi wound through the Heathrow tunnel at little more than walking pace. As the car emerged to greet the English scene, Fenton settled back in his seat, relaxed a little and even allowed himself a smile. Although his adopted home was Italy, he always felt an emotional tug whenever he visited the UK. And with this return, after the violence and threats of the last few days, Fenton also felt great relief at touching home ground – where everything seemed decent, familiar and well-ordered.

Still on the Heathrow feed road, the taxi overtook a couple of other cars. A glance behind told Fenton that no other vehicle had done the same. As the traffic thinned out and the cab picked up speed, he concluded, with some inner celebration, that he had indeed made a clean getaway from the airport. Only experienced criminals, political activists and spies would bother to think otherwise. Larry Fenton was none of these.

He was right of course to assume that he had been accompanied on the flight. However, most of those involved were not particularly concerned by his unbeatable departure from Customs. This was for several very good reasons all of which escaped Fenton's notice when he was still in the terminal building.

As they approached the main road, the cab driver slowed a little, and looked over his shoulder.

'Where to, guv – up the ortobarn?'

Lovely. Home and safe.

*

When there was no reply to his first telephone call that morning, it had merely seemed a minor setback. But as the day wore on with still no result, it became more of an endurance test. By early evening, Fenton had visited a score of West London snack bars and tea rooms. He had walked round many shops, department stores and picture galleries;

he had even spent half an hour in a cinema, but left when he found himself unable to stay awake. A dozen times he dialled Joanna's number – the same one he had called briefly from Hong Kong. He even checked in the directory: there it was, under 'Waley, J. 5 Rutland Gate, SW7'.

At 6.30 p.m. he gave up. He found a garage in the Brompton Road where he hired a car. The very act of doing something positive helped to relegate tiredness, and at least stabilise his growing impatience and frustration. Why, why – on this of all days – was Joanna not at home! True, she had told him in that call from Hong Kong that she might be 'out and about', but still ...!

After a few minutes' driving, getting used to the old Ford Cortina, Fenton settled for the idea that a few hours, one day even, would not make any real difference – so why not drive quietly down to Dorset and spend the night at the cottage?

In the heavy evening traffic, he floundered around in Clapham and Wandsworth, but eventually found his way onto the M3 at Sunbury.

The motorway seemed safe, part of the English scene and very different from the Italian free-for-all in which he usually lived. It also seemed comfortably remote from the threatening events of the last forty-eight hours. The car radio worked and the news bulletins had nothing about Hong Kong, Peking or, for that matter, about him – the fugitive Fenton.

Despite some initial misgivings about the condition of the car, it was humming along nicely and Fenton had to open a window to let in some breeze, to keep him from dozing off at the wheel. The Camberley exit came and went and then he was at junction seven, the turn-off for Basingstoke. Another twenty minutes would see him off the motorway and onto the A30 for Salisbury and Blandford Forum.

The events of the past few days played out in his mind. So far, he felt that he had come out of the affair pretty well. He had made some mistakes, but he thought that he had regained a sort of overall control. The only thing – and terrifying at that – was poor Jack Harper ...

Some miles before Blandford, he turned the car down a minor road leading to Chudmore, a tiny village on the edge of Cranborne Chase. It was a sparsely populated arable area, wooded in part but with no real forest. The area had no particular appeal for Fenton; it was more the preferred country of his father from whom he had inherited the cottage.

Chudmore was not a postcard-pretty hamlet, but it was neat and unspoiled. Among the isolated, simple huddle of buildings there was folklore cherished by the locals, but nothing that would attract most tourists. The main centre of activity was the Crown Inn. Fenton pulled up outside, a little after 10 p.m.

'Good to see you again, Mr Fenton – whisky? No Black Label, I'm afraid. Haig, Teachers ...'

'How are you, Fred? Anything will do, the day I've had. A large one, please.'

Fenton looked round. The three or four others in the bar nodded, muttered greetings. They were all vaguely familiar locals who Fenton only ever saw here, in the Crown.

In the small, low-ceilinged room an open fireplace was boarded up and fitted with one of those dark, bollard-shaped iron stoves. The vents were open and it was burning brightly. The old beams and other woodwork were painted in the interests of wear rather than to attract the eye. There were no brasses, bits of copper or farm implements hanging on the walls, as one might expect, and the decoration was minimal. There were just a few pictures of local scenes, a dartboard and a series of framed photographs of the apparently oft-winning Chudmore village cricket team. It was perhaps a little drab for a country pub, but it had a certain cosiness that Fenton appreciated.

'That'll be one forty.'

Fred, the landlord, wiped the counter and flipped a mat under the glass. Heavily built, balding and an ex-REME sergeant, he had been there for twenty years, but still wasn't considered a local.

'My God, that's expensive,' said Fenton, genuinely shaken.

'You're right,' Fred shrugged and smiled cheerfully, 'Like everything else these days.'

'What will you have, Fred?' Fenton asked. It was the usual, almost expected gesture.

'Oh, thank you, sir – I'll top up this.' He pulled some bitter into a half-empty glass. 'So you're here for the cottage, I suppose?'

Tired, preoccupied and comfortably off guard, Fenton absorbed the remark as merely a question phrased a little wrongly. Then Fred added: 'I didn't know it was up for sale until today ... G'night Jack, thanks. The wife says we could do with some eggs tomorrow ... 'night Denny, thanks.'

As he spoke, two farm workers whacked their empty tankards on the counter and nodded their farewells.

It was if somebody had dribbled ice-cold water down Fenton's spine. He clasped his glass in two hands and studied it intently. He was digging the thumb of his right hand into the palm of the left. He increased the pressure until it broke the skin.

'Yes,' he said finally. 'Where did you hear that, Fred?' It required a great effort of will for Fenton to speak normally.

'Well, the agents, Clapham's or something – never heard of 'em – was around here asking this morning. They couldn't even find the place. Don't know how you think you're going to sell it!'

*

Tucked away in a winding lane, the cottage was less than half a mile away. A thin, low cloud curtain over the night sky let through enough moonlight for the main shapes and surrounds of the cottage to be visible. Fenton drove slowly past, without stopping. The Cortina's headlights played over the thick hawthorn hedge that confined the front garden.

Everything seemed normal; the wooden gate in the hedge was closed, as was the larger one leading to the garage. From the brief glimpse of the buildings themselves, he could see nothing unusual. But then, he asked himself, what would there be to see?

He drove on carefully for two hundred yards until he reached a T-junction. He turned the corner and pulled up in a lay-by, parking the car behind a mound of Dorset County Council gravel destined for roadworks. He got out and moved a few paces onto the road. Looking behind, he was satisfied that, behind the pile of gravel, the Cortina was not immediately visible to passing cars. He then walked quietly back along the verge towards the cottage.

One moment he was thinking that these were absurd manoeuvres – especially in the vicinity of his own house in the English countryside – and the next he was seized by the same prickling fear that he had felt for much of the last few days.

By the time he reached the hedge, Fenton's eyes had become accustomed to the dark, although he was still thankful that he was on familiar ground. The wooden gate swung open with the same squeak, which became more pronounced with each visit. Fenton had forgotten about the noise of the gate, and swore softly. But he was careful to avoid the shingle path leading to the front door. He cut across the lawn and then round through the remains of a vegetable garden towards the rear of the cottage.

Everything seemed impossibly overgrown, even though he paid a man to come around and tidy up once a month.

The back door was protected by a half-windowed, timbered porchway. A waist-high interior ledge was home to sundry pots, small garden tools, balls of string, seed packets – the usual trappings of a potting shed. An old tobacco tin on the shelf housed the key to the door.

Fenton opened up and his hand groped on the wall towards the mains switch.

Normally, the electricity supply was left cut off. Although he was half prepared for it, Fenton's breath still caught in his throat when he found the switch already pulled down to the 'on' position.

The kitchen light also served a short passage that led directly to the front door. Fenton walked slowly through. Then he stopped, staring at a table to one side of the door. Propped against an anonymous Edwardian bronze bust was a neat stack of paper. It was the sort of thing that is thrust through letterboxes even when the postman is on holiday – brochures, parish newsletters, advertisements and the like. Fenton always found this junk mail scattered on the floor.

He jumped, startled at the sound of his own telephone in the living room. He knew that it happened, he had read about it and seen it in films, but not once in his life had Larry Fenton deliberately left a telephone ringing. It was an old installation, and the noise it made was a low and weary burbling. Scarcely had it stopped when Fenton again heard something familiar. This time it was outside. It was the squeaking front gate. Then there was the crunch of feet on the gravel.

Fenton froze for only a second. In a confused mixture of decision and alarm, he rushed back to the kitchen and flicked off the light. But what about a weapon of some sort? He groped towards a rack of utensils and pulled out a 9-inch kitchen knife. Then he let himself out quietly, raced across the vegetable patch and clambered over a fence into the adjoining field. He dashed from one clump of bramble to another until he found a ditch, which provided enough cover to get back to the lane. He reached the hedge and stopped, holding his breath to listen.

Somebody was stumbling around in the bushes not far behind him. He tentatively edged away and then dropped to the ground when he heard a man's muffled cough no more than a few yards away, further down the lane.

A second later there were more footsteps on the road and a brief glow of a light quickly extinguished. The visitors were so close that Fenton could hear one of them breathing heavily.

'We've lost him, then.' It was a panting half-whisper.

'He can't have got far – he can't fly.'

'I tell you, I didn't expect that! Something bloody funny's going on!'

'Ssh – not so loud.'

One of the men's voices betrayed a sort of panicky, frightened excitement that didn't sound quite right to Fenton. It was perhaps this which prevented him from surging forward at once and announcing his presence. The voices were comfortingly British, and for a second he considered getting up and asserting his rights. Why in heaven's name should he be crawling around in the Dorset countryside – why should he be running away from his own house and ...? His thoughts were cut off by more soft muttering from the prowlers:

'Ten yards away – I swear that's all! I swung my light on him. He was just standing there, dead still, this Chink – a bloody Chinaman – over there in that field of beet. I was a bit slow – well, for crissake, nasty shock it was – and he just vanished ... like that – I even—'

'Quiet. What's that?'

'There! Somebody crossed the lane up there ... I've got him now. He's slipping along, tight in against the hedge.'

'I see him. Right, we'll sort that out!'

Fenton heard some slight movement; then there was complete silence for a few seconds. Suddenly, one of the men shouted: 'Oi, you! Stop where you are!'

Two loud cracks in quick succession from a pistol answered the challenge. One round bounced off the road and whined away into the night. Only yards from Fenton's nose, the bushes crashed and sagged as the two men flung themselves down.

After a second's silence, a shocked, ragged voice said: 'Jesus, Len, this is real – we're being shot at!'

'Keep still – and watch, for God's sake!'

'I can't see anything. The bastard's moved away.'

'Come on, we'd better move up on him.'

'Len, wait – you're crazy! I tell you, I don't like this at all. I don't want to get killed for God only knows what reason in bloody Chudley.'

'Chudmore.'

'Whatever. We'll never get near him – and he won't be alone. Chinamen don't come in ones, they come in hordes.'

'I know – I was in Korea. Keep your head down and follow me.'

'What if he jumps us?' The voice was a barely audible croak from a dry throat.

Fenton didn't really need to listen to somebody else being frightened as well. He slid slowly away, cutting across the fields to the B road where he had left the car.

He pulled the driver's door open. The interior light cast an unwelcome pall of light around and also flashed on the kitchen knife still in Fenton's hand. He cursed, threw the knife onto the passenger seat, and then fumbled in pocket after pocket for the car keys. Sod it all – in all the floundering around he had lost them!

Fenton closed the door carefully and slumped in the seat. What to do? Could he get out of Chudmore on foot, without being bushwhacked by somebody of *any* nationality? As he sat there, debating whether to go cross country, or try and flag down a car on the main road, the cloud cover briefly exposed the almost full moon. The pale light struck the steering column, with the car keys glinting in their place. Fenton took a long, deep breath and let it out slowly. 'Good God ...' he muttered to himself. He started up, and drove quietly away.

After five or six miles he reached the top of a long hill, which he knew well. Fenton stopped the car and turned off the engine. He got out and looked back, listening for any signs of pursuit. There was none and, from that vantage point, Fenton could be absolutely sure that his was the only vehicle at the top of the vast slope of furrowed fields bordering on Cranbourne Chase. He reached back into the car, grabbed the knife, and threw it into the roadside ditch. If, given the forces ranged against him, he was actually driving into a stop-and-search, he thought that a 9-inch knife on the passenger seat wouldn't look good.

He motored on and not long after midnight he saw the lights of the High Cross transport café on the A303 a few miles outside of Andover. He was crumpling at the wheel. His eyes would no longer stay open for more than a few seconds at a time.

At least a dozen long-distance lorries were encamped in the café area. Fenton managed to thread the Cortina through the cluttered parking lot. Usually of threatening appearance, the monster trucks now seemed to provide solid walls of protection. Fenton found a place well away from the road; he had Charterhouse Frozen Foods on one side and Haulage Inter on the other. He switched everything off, locked himself in, and within a minute, was huddled into a deep and much-needed sleep.

*

'Back up your little affair, mate, will you – I've got to get my bus out!

The rap on the window woke him instantly. He gave a startled gasp and sat up. An unshaven face peered at him from inches away. The shoulder-length hair was parted down one side by an ear with a large gold ring in the lobe.

Fenton looked through the windscreen and saw that he was right in front of something of awesome dimensions with 'Scammel' emblazoned across the width of the massive radiator. He nodded and groped uncertainly for the ignition. There was another bang on the window. Fenton wound it down roughly.

'What is it?' he said. It sounded aggressive.

'Drink this cuppa first, mate – make you feel better.'

To Fenton's amazement, a hefty fist was pushing a mug of tea through the window. He took the mug and studied the contents. It seemed to be genuine transport-cafe tea.

'Well, thanks ...' Fenton looked blank, confused.

'Had a night out, did you?' the man said, with a grin. 'Looked bloody plastered when you came in – weaving in and out of the rigs. Lucky the Boot didn't get you – they patrol this stretch most nights.'

    'Thanks anyway. How much do I owe you?'

    'Pay Alf at the counter.'

sixteen

'LARRY, COME IN, come in!'

Fenton drew a deep chestful of air – and a trace of Givenchy's Ysatis – and then let it out again in an expansive gesture of relief. If, for days, he had done nothing but look over his shoulder, his gaze was now straight ahead at an attractive woman standing in the doorway of the second-floor flat at 5 Rutland Gate, and holding out both hands in greeting. She was a tall, forty-year-old, with long fair hair. Old and worn close-fitting beige jeans described a slim form. Fluffy slippers and a loose cotton blouse completed the relaxed appearance. With it all, was a certain poise that sometimes comes to those in the public eye. Joanna Waley was at home.

After a warm embrace of old friends, Joanna hung both hands around Fenton's arm and propelled him gently down the hallway. She was leaning lightly against him as they walked; the touch was light on his arm, but a flicker of excitement shot through Fenton as he felt it.

'It's lovely to see you, Larry – even if you do look a bit off-colour. Are you all right?'

'Yes. I'm just desperately tired. How about you, Jo?'

'Of course. I'm fine – as usual.' She smiled and squeezed Fenton's arm more firmly.

'I tried to phone when I got in yesterday, but you weren't around.'

'Gosh, yes … So sorry. I was out all day. Boring work for some publicity—'

'No problem, Jo, but the important thing … Tell me, has it arrived – the packet?'

'Yes, yes – this morning,' Joanna said, dismissing it with a wave of an elegant, cared-for hand. 'Come and sit down and we'll have a little something. I've got some whisky – not your sort, but … well, you've been away a long time, Larry. Let's get settled and you can tell me all about yourself.'

She looked straight at Fenton with large grey-blue eyes and smiled again.

They went into the lounge, separated from the dining room by a sliding glass partition. Apart from the latter, it was an old-fashioned décor. The furniture all seemed noticeably upright. Collector's pieces on spindly legs, a French writing desk and an eighteenth-century walnut bureau would have warmed the heart of any auctioneer. One wall was almost entirely filled by a tall Victorian glass-fronted book cabinet. The easy chairs had shoulder wings with cushions piled against the leather backing and the long canapé in front of the fire was also upholstered in leather. It was altogether a mannish room, more of a study than a drawing room.

'Where is it? asked Fenton.

'Through there – where it's always been.'

'I mean the packet.'

'Oh, that ... Heavens, Larry, you *are* in a state! Here, right under your nose.'

Fenton followed her glance and saw that the item that had involved him in so much turbulence in recent days was remarkably well displayed, propped up against an ornate guilt clock on the mantelpiece.

'Good God,' he mumbled. He retrieved the envelope, fingering it absent-mindedly, but with evident affection. 'Look, Jo, I'm not really able even to think straight at the moment, let alone explain anything. My brain is going funny with tiredness. May I sleep for an hour, and then I'll try and explain everything.'

'Larry, my poor darling – of course you can.' Joanna turned suddenly to face him. She held both his arms as if he were about to collapse. Fenton tucked the envelope into a pocket.

'What are you going to do with that?'

'Sleep on it.'

'If you take your shoes off, you can use my bed.'

'I hadn't counted on that.'

Fenton thought that he had smiled. Joanna, looking at him closely, could see nothing but the strained, drawn face of a man badly in need of proper rest. Fenton walked slowly through to the bedroom.

'I'll come and tuck you up in a minute. Do you want me to wake you later?'

'Yes please. Give me a couple of hours and then I'll be fine.'

Fenton dropped his jacket on a chair, removed his tie and eased off his shoes. He slid the envelope under the pillow and pulled the bedcover over him.

In the event, Joanna made an occasional check on the patient without disturbing him. Fenton eventually woke by himself. He had slept through until the early evening.

An open fire in the lounge was burning cheerfully with some smokeless fuel. A trolley loaded with an assortment of food for an armchair meal had been left at the side of the canapé. Also drawn up to hand was a small table on which stood a silver ice bucket, complete with a bottle, which gleamed with promise.

Emerging from the bedroom, Fenton took it all in with an appreciative smile made all the wider by the huge sense of relief at being out of harm's way.

'Are you feeling better, you poor boy?' Joanna came out of the kitchen, wiping her hands on a cloth, 'I just couldn't wake you – you looked as if you needed all the sleep you could get.'

'Marvellous – restored to full vigour. Was it you who took my clothes off?'

'Well, there's nobody else here.'

'Extraordinary. And I slept right through it ...'

'I've simply done a fireside snack – cold chicken, some salad, that sort of thing. Oh, and some soup. Is that all right? And there's a bottle of Sauvignon cooling off – would you like to open it? I can find some red plonk for the cheese.' She went off to the kitchen again.

Fenton opened the bottle and poured two glasses, which

he carried to the kitchen.

'Lovely, darling.' Joanna took a quick sip, kissed Fenton on the cheek and returned the glass to his hand. 'Take it back – I'm coming in with the soup.'

'Ah ... okay.' He returned to the fireside.

They were soon well installed on the canapé, ready to tuck into the snack Joanna had thrown together. The glasses clinked.

'I'm so glad to see you again, Larry.' Joanna's hands fluttered around on the trolley, found a napkin and gave it to Fenton. 'Right ... Now you're settled and refreshed, what have you been up to?'

Fenton put his glass down and bent to the leek soup. 'This is excellent,' he said.

'It comes from a packet. Now, let's go. Tell me all about it between mouthfuls.'

'Well, you see, I decided to take this couple of weeks' holiday in Hong Kong ...'

*

'But Larry, that's marvellous.'

Joanna leaned towards the dumb-waiter on wheels to pick up a small silver coffee pot. It was a simple piece with an engraved coat of arms on the side, partly effaced through wear. Fenton was offering his cup again.

'And what a story – you'll be famous and no doubt a lot richer as well.'

Fenton dropped an irregularly shaped lump of brown sugar into the cup, teasing at it with a tiny silver filigree spoon. He was staring at the cup, but saw nothing of what he was doing.

'Yes, it would be nice ...' he said slowly, '... but rich? I don't know – it's not about that any more, even if it was a consideration at the start. After what happened to Jack Harper, no amount of money would make me drop the story.'

'I know quite a lot of people who matter in the press

here. There are two or three on the posh Sundays who I know can be trusted. I'm sure they would jump at the chance to help.

'Jo, there are two problems. The first is that I'm not known here – and I'm obviously no sort of China expert. I would be pushed aside and lose control of the thing. I could see the way it was going in Hong Kong with that specialist *Review* magazine. Now, the second difficulty, even before negotiations, is that the authorities would kill the story. That D-Notice system still applies, doesn't it?'

'Yes, I think so, but it affects British secrets or security or something. What happens in Peking has got nothing to do with that.'

Joanna had her hand on Fenton's knee and she was looking at him with big, soft grey eyes that shone from a face that showed just enough small lines to make it interesting. Fenton sighed. He still found Joanna a beautiful and exciting woman.

'That MI5 man in Hong Kong, Marriot – he only had one leg, but he wasn't daft. I thought about it a lot later, going over our "meeting". He asked me, quite politely, to hand over the film and, moreover, he was making noises about payment. I refused and he simply let me walk onto the plane. And even the CIA was there with him.'

Fenton sighed and drained his coffee cup. 'This is good – much better than the black sludge in Italy.'

'It's instant, would you believe? The small cups make it taste better.' Joanna had the refill pot at the ready.

'Thanks. Yes, surprising – that American, Joe Streetman or something – he was quite civilised. Of course, it's clear to me now. Marriot was cleverly shoving me on home – home where they were all ready to receive me.'

'Larry, are you sure you're not getting a little bit of a persecution complex? After all—'

'For God's sake, Jo,' Fenton stood up, very agitated, 'there were at least two – probably more – British policemen, or something of that ilk, chasing me around the Dorset countryside. I know – I heard them two yards from my nose while I was lying in a bloody ditch! And the Chinese – they're here, too. *Everybody*'s after me. And there were bullets flying around. I'm not making this up!'

'Yes, all right, you poor man.'

'You can't tell me it's a coincidence that one of those police characters, scared to death, was telling his mate about a nimble Chinaman – there one minute, gone the next. This is *Dorset*, England! I don't know if it was the Chinese firing, the Russians or whoever ...'

Fenton's voice trailed off as Joanna started to laugh. He looked at her, nodded and made a grimace that was a parody of a smile.

'Yes, I know, it might seem comic.' There was some sarcasm in his voice. 'That man bleeding away in the hotel Gents, finding my room searched, playing cops and robbers ever since ... Even getting bashed on the head, apparently by Russians, might sound amusing in retrospect. But, believe me, Jo, it made me feel bloody ill for a good few hours.'

'I know. I'm sorry, Larry. It all seems just so ... fantastic? I don't know the right word. Surreal? And you *do* make it sound a bit comic!'

'Well, okay, I guess a lot of it does look far-fetched. But the whole thing becomes less hilarious when you know that an Australian journalist, mistaken for me, was murdered in Hong Kong. Moreover, those were *real* shots in the night, bang outside my back door – in rural Dorset, goddammit! Even the policemen were peeing in their pants. All right, there were perhaps a few moments when I thought I was having fun. Now it's different.'

He pushed his legs out and leant back on the canapé. He instantly regretted the outburst. Perhaps he could have made the point with less vehemence, but it was a reaction to what he sensed to be Joanna's doubts about all that he had recounted in his usual low-key, bland style.

'Yes, I know, Larry. It's awful. Don't fret. I'll get you a whisky.'

Joanna coaxed the trolley, laden with the wreckage of the finished meal, into the kitchen. She came back a minute later with a lacquer tray on which there were a couple of finely cut half-tumblers, a small water jug from the same French crystal house and a bottle of competitive Scotch from a supermarket.

'I'll find an editor tomorrow who will get round your D-Notice business, and anyway there's always Freddie at the Home Office – he does more or less what I tell him. Water? Say when.'

'Listen, Jo – thanks, that's enough. But this thing is at a different sort of level. It's not something that can be arranged by influence, even yours. These Security people are not on my back for no reason at all. They'll do everything to try to stop me even getting *near* an editor's office.'

'What do you want to do, then?'

'Don't see there's a choice. No journalist would hesitate. And I've never before had such a chance. I need a bit of time to think straight, so that I don't make any more mistakes.' Fenton smiled grimly.

'For the first time in a week, I'm not in somebody's sights. Nobody can possibly know where I am. I was all by myself last night on the Dorset downs. I even pulled in for a few hours at a transport cafe.'

'A transport ... Good lord!'

'Coming here,' Fenton continued, 'it wasn't really necessary, but I was dead careful. I left the car somewhere in south London, and called the hire garage, telling them the battery was flat.'

With some satisfaction, Fenton elaborated a little with other details of his developing skills at evasion. But he became aware that he had lost the attention of Joanna who seemed suddenly subdued. Concern had wrinkled its way onto her face. She stood up, tapping a fingernail lightly against an empty coffee cup. She walked away.

Fenton watched, entranced, as the tall, trim figure moved to a window. Joanna pulled back the curtain an inch and looked down at the street.

'More film footage has been shot of that scene than of

any other,' said Fenton cheerfully. 'So what do you see?'

'Nothing unusual.'

The curtain dropped back into instant order, in the way that heavy velvet does. Joanna turned to Fenton with a bright smile. Any glum thoughts had apparently fallen away with the curtain.

She sat down and wriggled under Fenton's arm stretched along the back of the cushions. He smiled, shyly, with a bit of guilt, and let his new-found sense of well-being take on another dimension.

'We could at least plot a bit, Larry. It's all tremendously exciting.'

'It was another mistake, of course,' Fenton mused, 'I thought England would be safer. It seemed to be the right place to launch the story. But in fact I would have been better off in Italy where I've got the immediate ear of editors, and no British security people trying to stop me. At least, I can't really believe that the long arm of—'

'But, Larry my sweet, Italy's a NATO country. What about the Italian government? Wouldn't they do the same as us? The police, I mean.'

Joanna kicked off her slippers and drew her legs up onto the seat. The movement nudged her more firmly against an already bolt-hard Fenton.

'It's different. Italian newspapers do much as they like.'

The tone had become casual, disinterested even. With the softest touch, the beleaguered Larry Fenton now found himself caressing the back of Joanna's head. His hand dropped back slowly over the nape. It was a gesture that brought back memories to both. Nothing much seemed to have changed.

Recent events had perhaps made him unusually vulnerable or sensitive. And there was indeed the safe haven aspect. Moreover, Joanna put a charge into him that he had never found with anybody else. He felt sumptuously turned on and Joanna stirred and flexed like a pampered cat.

'Funny thing ... It all went wrong from the start. Almost as if life, other people, were conspiring to stop young Larry getting his lucky break. I got things wrong, but I don't see what anybody else would have done in my place. The last bad mistake was coming to England. For crissake, I could have gone anywhere! But the homing instinct took over, I suppose.'

'You're a very sweet man, Larry,' Joanna said softly, 'And I'm glad you made your last mistake.' She reached up and feathered her fingers across his cheek.

'Do you think we might go to bed?' Fenton said with offhand certainty.

Joanna reached forward and kissed him fully on the mouth in a lingering way that sent him reeling back seven years, or was it eight?

'I thought you were never going to ask,' she said. Fenton smiled and groped for his glass.

'Give me five minutes. Have another whisky.' Joanna bounced away and Larry Fenton was left to stretch, yawn and reflect on what seemed to be a turn for the better after a rough week.

He heard a drawer being pulled open and then slammed shut. Then there was a clink of glass on a washbasin or bathroom shelf. Snatches from different radio programmes succeeded one another as Joanna was evidently trying to tune into something she wanted. Fenton recognised an impatient snort of old and the radio was switched off. The sound of running water lasted a few minutes and then that, too, stopped.

'Larry ...?'

Fenton sighed and stood up. He found a master switch on the wall that put out the lights in the main living area.

The bedroom was strikingly different in mood from the formality of the lounge. Long, flat dressers, with slim drawers, and finished in a slight off-white made irrevocable dents in the thick-piled lavender carpet. The bed, too, was a low-slung affair with no headboard; it was shouldered by fitted lockers with still more drawers. All the items had evidently been tailor-made for the room and the 'design' element made it clear this was not a suite you could buy off-

the-peg at a department store. Fenton, in fact, those years
ago, had known the designer, a London-based Italian friend
of Joanna's – of whom he was naturally suspicious.

The soft drapes were subdued pinks and mauves. Most
of half a dozen or so modern paintings, all saleable, were
hung by obligation. Some, Fenton knew, Joanna did not
appreciate particularly, but were in place because they were
contributions from artist friends.

Joanna was pulling a brush through her ash-blond hair
with one hand and pinning an ample, maroon coloured
towel round her with the other.

'You'll find all you want and another towel in the
bathroom.'

'I want that one,' said Fenton, pointing and advancing
towards Joanna.

'Oh come on, Larry – you're not ... Larry! Well ...'

The deftness was surprising, given his fatigue, but he
easily tweaked the towel free and it fell in a pile around
Joann's feet. She didn't move and Fenton stood there,
stunned.

'It's still as sensational as it ever was,' he said. He bent,
grabbed the towel and made for the bathroom without
looking back. On the way, his eyes fell on a small-framed
photograph on the dressing table. It was of a man but
Fenton was too far away to distinguish the features. Some
of his exhilaration disappeared at once.

It had always been the problem – the men around
Joanna. But it could hardly be otherwise. Rather than take
his chance eight years ago in what he regarded as an
unequal struggle, Fenton had shied away from Joanna
precisely because he concluded that she would never be his
exclusive property.

He took his time under the shower. He found a
toothbrush and electric razor laid out for his use. As Joanna
had said, everything he might want was there. He cleaned
his teeth, but for a bit of rebellion, left the razor untouched.
He draped the towel over some heated chrome rails and
went back into the bedroom, carrying his clothes.

Involuntarily he looked at the dressing table again. The photograph was no longer there.

Fenton eased himself into the bed. He pulled Joanna towards him and slid his hand down her long, supple back. The shock of the contact was delicious. For moments they didn't move.

There was perhaps less rumpling of the sheets and shouting than in earlier years but the result was the same. Joanna finally fell asleep in Fenton's arms. He wanted to stay awake longer, to savour and to think. But it didn't last long.

He slept soundly, but only for an hour or two. He was completely out of phase with European time and, despite all that Joanna had done to him, he was suddenly wide awake at 4.30 a.m.

A distant wall light left a dim, suffused glow over the comfortable, tender scene. Fenton's eyes ranged round the room for some minutes. Then he was looking very precisely at a small pile of clothes – delicate bits – that Joanna had thrown on a padded stool by the dressing table.

Fenton disengaged gently and slipped out of bed. A wry smile was on his face, and he bit his lower lip. He seemed to be forever stealing from the bed of the moment.

It was the corner of the frame that he had seen. Whatever they did for Joanna, the flimsies were not quite enough to hide the photograph. Feeling guilty and furtive, Fenton glanced back at the bed. Joanna was sleeping deeply.

Seconds later he crept under the covers again. He made countless attempts to get comfortable, lying first on one side and then on the other. He knew that it was hopeless. His mind was scrambling through a surfeit of ideas and memories. The fidgeting and perhaps a tug at the sheet had its effect. A warm hand groped over Fenton's belly.

'You're awake, Larry. What are you fretting about?' It was a muffled, languid noise.

'Yes, I'm so sorry, Jo. I suppose it's the time difference.'

She half propped herself up and sipped at a bedside glass of water. Then sinking down again, she turned to face Fenton.

'Darling man, I think I had better ask you something.'

'Yes?' Said Fenton, immersed in his own thoughts.

'Who is your lodger?'

Fenton screwed up his eyes and dragged his attention to the question.

'What lodger – what are you talking about?' He had a frown and a nonplussed smile on his face at the same time.

'The man at the cottage – the one who is staying there.'

The sheets suddenly seemed to be sticking to Fenton's naked flesh. He sat bolt upright in bed.

'Jo, what the hell are you talking about?'

'Yes, perhaps I should have brought it up earlier but I didn't really think about it and I suppose -'

'Get to the point, Jo!'

'Well, you see, when the package arrived yesterday morning, I ... I telephoned the cottage before I left early on the publicity thing. A very polite man said that he was staying there but that you were expected at any time and he could take a message.'

Fenton was staring at Joanna in dreadful fascination.

'Go on,' he whispered.

'That's it. I asked him to tell you to call me back.'

'And you gave your name!' Fenton had sprung out of bed and was already scrambling into his clothes.

'Well, I said it was Mrs Waley and ... yes, I know what it means; I gave him the telephone number. Don't be cross, Larry – how could I have known? You said nothing in the call from Hong Kong.'

Joanna sounded hurt but Fenton scarcely noticed. 'It's not a question of being cross. Men wearing raincoats will be thumping on the door before dawn even if they're not outside already waiting. Or else it will be the lot that eat noodles for breakfast!'

'But what ... what are you *doing* in such a rush?'

'I'm going to Italy.'

'At four o'clock in the morning?'

'If I don't leave now, I'll never make it.'

Fenton was already sitting on the bed lacing up his shoes with more haste and less precision than usual.

'That envelope represents a lot more than a happy retirement. I waited a long time for a really big story. This is it.' Fenton tapped his jacket pocket. 'No journalist would back off. Having got this far, I'll be damned if I'm going to give up just because this or that government doesn't want it published! And then there's Harper ...'

'Be realistic, Larry, for your own sake – you have already seen what they can do.'

'Right. And that's one good reason why I intend to go through with the bloody thing – come what may.'

He stooped in front of the dressing table mirror. There was silence for a moment while his nervous fingers produced an ungainly knot too far down the thin end of the tie. He cursed and whipped it from his neck. As he started fumbling away again, he felt his shoulders being turned.

'Let me do it.' Joanna said. Her hands reached out to his collar. 'It was a short night, Larry.'

Fenton didn't know what to say. He folded his arms around Joanna. For some moments he stared, unseeing, over her shoulder. The press has a duty to report the truth, doesn't it? If the prospect of recognition and money drove him at the start, it was now incidental. Competing questions and doubts bounced around in Fenton's mind. The word 'irresponsible' was there for a second, but was soon nudged away by an already well-installed stubborn reaction to the threats and pressure. And more than anything, his overall mood of defiance was governed by cold anger at Harper's murder.

Confusion lingered. Fenton drew back a little, gazing at Joanna's face, hands on her shoulders. She said nothing, but had that eyebrows-raised, chin-down look of doubtful inquiry that means *so what next?*

Fenton turned abruptly and his eyes cast round the room. There was something sane and well-ordered at

Rutland Gate, an atmosphere of abiding comfort and life as it should be led. And Joanna was in his arms. What's more, after all those years, she had kept a photograph of him, intimately, on her dressing table. Of course he couldn't be sure that it was there every day, but still ... With a puff of exasperation, Larry Fenton made a decision.

'Jo, we can spend some longer nights together – come with me to Rome!' he said suddenly.

'Now?'

'Yes, why not? It would be ... well, it would be nice.' It came out like that – an absurdly unattractive way to put the proposition. Fenton cast around in his mind for a better formula. Before he could speak again, Joanna had detached herself from him and started dressing with the speed only seen backstage at a fashion show.

'Nice?' she was saying. 'What the hell does that mean – with you on the run like this! And I've got a broadcast next week.'

'You'll be back by then, I promise.'

'I'm counting on you to make this a memorable and worthwhile trip.'

'I'll try,' said Fenton, smiling. His suggestion hadn't been planned; it just emerged as a sudden impulse. He felt a great wave of comfort. Joanna's presence in Italy for a few days would mean a certain support that he desperately needed. It wasn't exactly a heroic attitude perhaps, and at the back of his mind was the honest recognition that not being alone counted as much as the prospect of spending some longer nights together.

They left by a rear entrance that gave access to a fire escape zigzagging down the wall of the building. A narrow passage behind continued along the back of another block, from where a narrow lane led to the main street.

At that hour it was still dark and quiet except for a thin background murmuring of scattered and distant traffic.

When they reached the corner where lane met street, Fenton suddenly bundled Joanna into a doorway. A small shadowy movement nearby had caught his eye, and then a metal dustbin lid clattered onto the path, with the noise booming and echoing off the surrounding brickwork. A scavenging cat scuttled away.

They walked on a few yards. Fenton heard the car even before it turned slowly round the corner at the end of the street. He pulled Joanna back into the entrance to the lane.

'Wait.'

'Larry, I think we should just walk quietly away.' Joanna huddled against him, tugging at his arm.

'No. Let's watch for a moment. I think the raincoats have arrived.'

The car stopped and two people got out. They sauntered along on the opposite side of the road. One was looking up at Joanna's flat where, at Fenton's last-second insistence, a visible light had been left on. The man was not wearing a raincoat; it was an anorak or similar with the collar turned up. He stopped, yawned and tapped a folded newspaper against his mouth while staring up at the window. His companion, of much the same style, walked on twenty yards and sat down on the concrete base of some iron railings outside another block of flats. The car reversed a length or two and then its lights were switched off.

'My God, Larry, what are you getting me into – are you sure you've told me everything?'

'Come on, we'll go back a bit and get out onto another street.'

They walked for ten minutes, which seemed a lot longer, until they were halfway along Knightsbridge.

'There's one.' Fenton waved, and the taxi pulled up.

'Heathrow, please.'

'Streuth ...!' muttered the driver and glanced at his watch in disbelief. 'You're on standby, are you?'

It was a little after five in the morning.

seventeen

ONCE, IT MUST HAVE been an elegant, if isolated, residence. The villa looked run-down, crumbling, and to a casual observer, it could even have been abandoned. Half a mile away, an undulating line of electricity pylons pegged the closely wooded slopes into place. This was the nearest obvious evidence, apart from the rough track, of civilisation. Astonishingly wild, the area was less than half an hour's drive north of Rome, at the foot of the Umbrian hills.

It was a brilliantly clear day, the air still, and pleasantly warm. The faded pastel colours of caking plaster-wash on the walls produced a dappled camouflage effect among the shadows and sunlit foliage.

They had seen the car in the distance when it was still in the valley, crawling through the vegetation like some shiny, black bug. Minutes later they heard the Alfetta arrive at the bottom of the track. Doors slammed and the car was manoeuvred to be pointed back carefully in the direction from which it had come. The engine was then switched off.

A man left his observation post and hurried up towards the villa, using the stunted trees and scrub as cover. He was a thirty-year-old Italian, slightly built, wearing jeans, a cheap mud-coloured T-shirt with a button-up neck and plastic sandals. His face, pale and intense, was dramatised by a heap of black hair sprouting from under a dark-blue seafarer's cap. He was nervous, soon out of breath from the short climb, and he'd never been to sea in his life. He pushed open the main door of the villa.

'There are three coming up. One is still in the car, maybe more; I can't tell because the windows are dark ...' he paused to take in air '... tinted,' he added, finding the right word in English.

The message provoked some immediate movement.

People seemed to know exactly what to do and where to go.

The interior of the villa was roughly furnished and equipped, but in much better repair than the outside would have suggested. One noticeable feature was that, although many of the wooden shutters were broken or rotting, the windows inside were reinforced with new metal screens. Although not a real security system, it would be enough to deter any casual break-in.

Another remarkable aspect was the presence of the Financial Director of a British firm in Hong Kong. A long way from his distinctly grand Peeble Hunt office, a shirt-sleeved Gerry Tan was sitting at a small table under a window in the main room of the villa. With one hand, he was playing with the dials and switches on two slabs of equipment, each the size of a large cornflakes packet; his other hand clasped one of the horseshoe earphones to the left side of his head. He looked more like a laboratory worker than a high-powered executive, and he was evidently practised with the WT set-up.

Tan's uncovered right ear took in the panted-out news about the arrivals, while he used hand gestures to deploy people to the adjoining and upper level rooms.

He put down the earphones, adjusted a frequency lock and then the volume control; this left a faint hiss from a built-in speaker in one of the boxes. He went to the door to await the visitors.

He had not wanted to run the operation like this, but he wouldn't have been able to find Chinese resources in the time for such a job. The Englishman, Fenton, had unfortunately turned out to be tricky or stupidly obstinate – or both; even his own people evidently couldn't control him. The logic was to go for his vulnerable spot. There had been several possibilities. One, unexpected, was now the imperative choice.

Three men walked out of the scrub towards the clearing in front of the villa. There was nothing exceptional in the appearance of two of them: one had his sports jacket thrown over his shoulder; another was neatly unencumbered in a pink open-neck shirt and permanently pressed beige Tergal trousers.

The third man was different. There in that bucolic setting, the well-tailored three-piece dark blue suit was eye-catching. Moreover, the elegance persisted despite an unbuttoned white shirt and lack of tie.

Tan, waiting with folded arms at the door, took it all in. At twenty yards, the general style of the man in the suit was obvious. As he came closer, something else became clear. Tan stiffened. It was bizarre. The man approaching him wore a child's clip-on false face of dark glasses, nose and moustache.

Tan moved slightly to one side and beckoned the party to come into the villa. By the door, the besuited man lifted first one foot and then the other, flicking the dust off his highly-polished shoes with a handkerchief. Then he went inside. One of his companions followed closely behind; the other remained outside.

'Ask him if he wants to take a look round first,' said Tan, turning to his pale, dark-eyed interpreter with the plastic sandals.

'I am speaking enough English,' said the man in the mask. He made a dismissive gesture with his hand towards the young Italian. 'Yes, I take a quick look over.'

He muttered something to his companion and moved quickly into the next room and from there into the kitchen. Then he climbed halfway up an open wooden staircase from where he could see into some of the floor above. His feet remained on a step at eye-level with those below. Tan noticed the dark red silk socks – just right for the shine on the shoes.

'That's a lot of Chinese in one small villa – I don't see all the rooms and I don't count those outside in the trees.'

The visitor fingered his bulbous *papier mâché* nose and sat down on a chair with its back pushed against the newly plastered wall.

Tan opened his hands as if gently launching an invisible balloon; it was that slight, patient gesture of 'that's the way it is'.

'Can you do it?' he said.

'What is *that?*' The Italian, pointed to the WT equipment on the table. For a second or two, Tan stared blandly at the mask.

'My communications. I prefer not to use the telephone.'

'Turn it off.'

'Certainly not – it could take a quarter of an hour to retune,' said Tan quietly. 'There are a few other things to worry about. And you seem to be forgetting where you are. These are Chinese premises ...'

The Italian turned to his assistant. What would have no doubt been an obvious expression of facial inquiry was hidden by the ludicrous mask.

'Stefano,' he snapped, 'What about that?'

Thick arms suddenly bunched together and the shoulders were humped into a shrug; a squat face peeked forward and the corners of the mouth dragged down. Stefano didn't want to commit himself.

'Can you do it?' Tan said again.

The Italian got up and walked to the doorway. He stood staring outside for some moments. He looked at the clear blue sky; he kicked lightly at the dusty rubble on the path and waited for any comment from his other helper posted by the door. There was none.

'No problem, no problem.' He came back and drew up a chair to sit opposite Tan. 'You put half down and we get started—'

'Pasquali said a third,' said Tan sharply, 'and that's in hand already.'

'Pasquali, Pasquali – okay! But he's not doing ...' The Italian put a finger to his head. It could have been a pistol or it could have been pointing to brainwork. 'You know about Pasquali, yes? Anyway, I tell you something. We have an arrangement, okay. Sometimes it's like that. Right now they need money. Pasquali is not using his Group people in business where they get no political *beneficio,* no propaganda. *Capito?* Too much risk. And they recently lost a lot of people. So we have good arrangement. Okay, start is easy – like collecting laundry down the road. We make it look like GAP for the benefit of this *inglese*. Then we gotta act careful – making sure the guy behaves right. Risk there costs money. No problem. But I fix the terms.'

'No haggling,' said Tan softly. 'We proposed a job to be done against payment conditions agreed with Pasquali. That's the deal.'

'Half down!' The Italian chopped the edge of one hand on the back of the other.

'No way. The arrangements have been made. Can't be changed now. The operation must get started later today. Delay means no deal.'

The Italian put his hands behind his head, flicking at the elastic that kept the mask in place.

'Think about it,' he said.

Tan filled his lungs slowly and then let the breath rush out with a fierce hiss of exasperation. He turned and fiddled with the WT, clapping an earphone to his head. He spent a few minutes in a rapid fire exchange while the principal visitor remained seated, motionless and listening in fascinated incomprehension. The other man put on his jacket for something to do, and then fell to staring at Tan's class-conscious interpreter who was perched on a corner bench and looking anxious. The young man had not so far been needed.

Suddenly there was silence. Everybody looked at Tan. He turned to the boss Italian and made his habitual open hand gesture.

'It's already been organised in Milan and Zurich. It is impossible to get further signatures today. And that amount of extra money can't be found in Rome.'

Tan leaned back in his chair and lit a cigarette. The smoke hung dense and grey in a shaft of sunlight; he flapped at it, and then stared at the visitor again.

'That's the scene,' he said, 'Sort it out with Pasquali. The operation starts now.' The tone was short and decisive.

He barked out something in Mandarin while looking

towards the top of the stairs. After some scuffling about above them, and the brief murmur of voices, a Chinese in a white shirt with the sleeves rolled up padded down the stairs quickly on splayed bare feet. He gave a fat buff envelope to Tan.

'I shouldn't think there would be too much "*beneficio*"...' Tan was smiling thinly, '... in getting into an argument with Pasquali and the Group.'

He looked briefly in the envelope.

'They may have had some setbacks, but they still have a lot of muscle, yes?'

'*Cosa?*'

The Italian had not followed.

'Never mind.' Tan tossed the envelope across to the other man.

'There's ten thousand extra that I don't have to tell Pasquali about.'

One hand nursed the packet while a finger of the other strayed up under the mask to scratch at a real nose. The Italian withdrew his finger, studied it carefully and then used it to lunge at the packet.

'What do I do with that – pay off my driver?' It must have been a standard, derisive joke in that milieu.

Tan's interpreter sniggered, and the other Italian visitor snorted; it was the latter's first audible contribution to the session. Tan looked round blandly.

'Which one stays with us?'

Seconds passed while the Italian thought it through. Then he lifted his head slightly in the direction of the one who had snorted.

'Stefano,' he said.

Tan immediately wrote something on a scrap of paper. He stood up and handed the note to the visitor. Then he gestured in the way of a host ushering out guests.

'You can call us on that number this afternoon. Your ... your Stefano will be in a position to confirm that payment has been made. Then you move. You have the rest of the day and tomorrow morning if necessary. The balance will be transferred after delivery – as agreed with Pasquali. And if you don't like—'

The Italian cut him short with a bored wave of the hand and he turned on his heel. On the way to the door, he stabbed a foreman's finger in Stefano's direction. He said nothing, but the message was clear: *You're on. Just get it right!*

Outside, the third Italian detached himself from the shade of some lush creeper overhanging the door and followed his boss. They had only gone a few yards when the clown mask whipped round. With some violence the man flung the envelope back at Tan standing in the doorway. The aim was bad and the packet thudded against the wall. The impact broke it open and an impressive number of bundles of US $100 bills scattered on the gravel.

'We gotta business deal – not a Chinese market!' He spoke loudly enough to be heard clearly, but without shouting. They went on down the track.

Tan stood there, impassive, watching them disappear into the scrub. He rather liked the style of the departure. One of his minions was scratching around the door gathering up the notes. A minute or two passed, and then Tan was thankful to hear the Alfetta leave quietly and not, as he half expected, with the motor screaming and gravel being spat back at the countryside. So that's the mafia on a contract job, he mused to himself.

*

The second party prepared to leave in a VW minibus. This vehicle was needed because, in addition to Tan, there were seven Chinese, the interpreter and the recent recruit, Stefano.

It was a long journey for the latter. He was a round, compact man, thickly built, but not really in good physical condition. Normally this was not important because he was skilled at close-range small arms work. This asset, however, seemed to him increasingly irrelevant as he found himself wedged in among a great deal of Chinese flesh for the best part of forty minutes.

He made several light-hearted attempts at conversation with those around him; this elicited head-shaking and Chinese smiles but not much else. He gave up. And he didn't feel socially able to engage with his one compatriot – the one with the Helmut Schmidt cap, long hair and plastic sandals, who was sitting up front with Tan and the driver.

Stefano was no fool. In his position, he couldn't afford to be. Probably every policeman in Rome had seen his photograph at one time or another, even if they didn't remember it. For most of the journey Stefano, without being asked, squatted on the floor of the VW minibus.

It was around 5.30 p.m. as they entered Rome's outer limits, so they encountered heavy traffic already building up for the rush hour chaos. The driver peeled off the Via Nomentana, an arterial road in the north of the city. He got lost in a maze of side streets but finally found his way into one of the so-called diplomatic quarters.

Via Bruxelles was the address that counted. It was nicely placed between two vast public parks, the Villas Borghese and Ada. The embassy was a four-storey yellow building of faded charm, set in enough ground to make it very private. The VW bumped into the driveway and steel gates clanged shut behind.

The bus accelerated and a made a squealing, tight turn round to the rear of the premises. They went down into the parking area under the building at such speed that it was clear even to Stefano that the driver now knew the way. They all got out, and most of the party filed up the stairs leading to the main embassy offices.

Tan, accompanied by the interpreter, went out again immediately by the front door. A Mercedes with diplomatic plates was waiting in the forecourt. The car had started to move towards the gates when a bespectacled Chinese in a blue tunic uniform rushed up and tapped on the window.

'The Ambassador wants to see you,' he panted. Tan glanced at his watch.

'I'll be back in less than an hour.'

The Mercedes slipped out to join Rome's ill-disposed, snarling traffic.

*

Gerry Tan was installed at a table in a pavement café at the Piazza Colonna. From there he could admire not only the spiralling thirty-foot high monument to Marcus Aurelius, but also the renaissance facade of the *Il Tempo* newspaper building. Tan reflected that it must be the only press headquarters in the world apparently held up by a score of neoclassical columns. He thought that he would try out this remark the next time he met a journalist.

'Get him out of there on any pretext. We can do it all in ten minutes. Probably less.'

Tan sipped at his cappuccino and watched the interpreter scurry across the square. He had barely time to review the company at surrounding tables – businessmen and tourists mainly – when the interpreter came back with another man. The latter, in his late thirties, was casually – almost scruffily – dressed; he looked like a junior office clerk or messenger.

'Toni ...' said the interpreter by way of introduction. They sat down. While the waiter fussed around taking orders, they were speaking English.

'It's hopeless. He's there all the time,' said Toni, 'I only see the frame I'm working on; nothing more. He takes the negative and the product away immediately.'

'How much have you done?'

'I've almost finished the third frame. I really can't delay things more. As it is, he's agitated at the slow pace and I think he's already complained about it upstairs. And of course, when the editor first called me in to do the job, he said it was urgent – and confidential. Given what it's about, not surprising they want it done quickly ...'

The waiter brought further coffees and tucked the bill under a saucer. When he had gone, the one called Toni, with amazing ease, switched to reporting in fluent Mandarin.

'The trouble is, it's not possible to fudge the issue – he speaks near perfect Italian, and he writes it better than I do.'

'All right,' said Tan. 'You're sure that he has no idea that we …' Tan tapped his chest. '… our Embassy, I mean … know about the work in hand?'

'Of course I'm sure!'

'Okay. The important thing is what does he do with the negatives?'

If the question had been asked in Mandarin, then the reaction was robustly Italian: hands all over the place and the face distorted into mournfulness of operatic scale.

'No idea. He's there when I arrive, and still around when I leave. Maybe he even sleeps there.'

'No, he doesn't do that,' said Tan quietly.

'He's got a pass, of course, giving him the run of the building. I guess he just packs the negatives away somewhere handy. Not exactly difficult to hide – left in a book or something. But they could be anywhere.'

'So there's no way to—'

'*Mei-yu.* None!'

'And where are you doing the work?'

'We're using the deputy editor's office. He's away until Monday.'

*

So ended a conversation in Mandarin at the Piazza Colonna in Rome. One of the participants was Antonio Pinelli – Toni – who was a good linguist, an expert on the Chinese economy and an ad hoc consultant to *Il Tempo*; he had never mentioned it in the newspaper offices, but he happened to be a member of the Sino-Italian Friendship Association, which people joined for a variety of reasons.

In his case, membership brought with it a kind of privileged and regular contact with local Chinese officials. From this link came the meeting with a certain G.T. Tan – a very particular 'official' visiting from Hong Kong and one who apparently could afford to keep the Chinese Ambassador waiting an hour.

*

Some of the charm and elegance of the drawing room had been lost in renovation. Whether out of particular taste or political orthodoxy, the original motif of the moulded frieze was painted out. An extravagant plaster floral design in the middle of the ceiling really called for a chandelier; instead, a single lamp of a banal modern design hung there. Dark brown curtains of heavy fustian were drawn over the windows. Although the rest of the soft furnishings – standard easy chairs and three sofas – were covered in a more expensive-looking beige material, the whole effect was mundane.

On two large tables were partly depleted bowls of cocktail biscuits, nibble sticks and piles of those so-called shrimp crackers that look like bits of foam rubber. Plates of sandwiches and some specifically Chinese morsels stuck together with toothpicks completed the buffet arrangement.

Crumbs on the table, half-empty glasses and tea slops showed that refreshments had already been served. A few of the embassy staff were scattered around, talking quietly in small groups – as if taking a break from usual office duties.

On arrival, for a brief moment, Stefano had taken the scene as a surprising show of hospitality for his benefit – as one of his Chinese minders ushered him to a table. He quickly realised that it was all merely a sort of staff bonus, and that the small chow was in fact leftovers from a reception earlier in the day. But he had gone about his task in good humour.

On one of the tables, among the buffet remnants, was a grey telephone that had been brought into the room and plugged in half an hour earlier. Stefano was seated, sweating, changing the receiver from ear to ear. It was hot in there. The air-conditioning had been switched off after the real reception, and the Italian, out of his element, as well as being keyed up, felt it more than the others. The receiver was wet in his grasp and occasional drops of sweat fell off the tip of his nose into the mouthpiece. He was engaged with his last call.

'*Va bene,* okay!' he announced to the room.

He dropped the phone and stood up, mopping his face and neck with an already soaked handkerchief. As he slung his jacket over his shoulder, he suddenly noticed Tan, standing by the glass-panelled door.

The Italian gestured with a fist full of handkerchief and turned to the interpreter:

'Tell him that it will be done tonight or tomorrow morning at the first chance.'

'Fine,' Tan nodded without waiting for the translation.

Stefano started towards the door, eager to leave. He stopped in his tracks. Tan was placed squarely in front of the exit, blocking his path.

'Make sure Stefano understands that he won't be leaving until after the delivery,' Tan said, directing his remark over Stefano's shoulder to the interpreter. 'He may be useful here.'

The interpreter shook some bunches of black hair from his face; his hands were at waist level holding the rim of his blue cap, which he was nervously manoeuvring like a steering wheel.

Stefano had understood even before the interpreter started. Everybody was still. The Italian's sodden handkerchief dropped to the floor with a soft plop.

'I leave now …' he said in a half whisper.

He was indeed slightly crouched, as if ready to take off. Nobody had seen how it had happened, but one of his short, sturdy arms had grown a little longer with the small pistol he was holding. It was only for a second. Alert, and adroit with the weapon he was, he had no time to round on everybody – or even to decide on priorities.

The moment his attention turned to Tan when the latter started to speak again, there was an irruption in the room. In a blur of sudden movement out of nowhere, Stefano had the impression of being hit in several places at the same time. His elbow was jarred limp and something chopped at his wrist causing the gun to fly from his hand; his legs were cut from under him, and he dropped to the floor. It was in total disbelief that he gazed up at his three blue-tunicked assailants. Stefano got to his feet again, but he didn't move further – except to rub his wrist.

Tan walked forward and picked up the gun, without sparing it a glance.

'Yes, you must stay here, because if anything goes wrong,' he said softly. 'You will be our liaison man with the police ...' Tan waited while this savagely perverse threat was translated and lodged in the Italian's mind. 'In reality, of course, your presence should ensure that nothing *does* go wrong.'

A short silence was ended by a series of briefly spaced and furious outbursts in Italian; it was as if Stefano was using a machine gun, which would not have been for the first time. Tan looked inquiringly at the interpreter. The latter had stuffed the cap into his waistband, and was gulping down the remains from somebody else's glass.

'He's not very happy,' he said and wiped his mouth.

Tan shrugged. He turned to Stefano, who was seething but impotent in the subtle grasp of two deceptively placid Chinese, one of whom had earlier served him green tea.

'Relax,' Gerry Tan said, 'You'll be all right here. Protected. This is diplomatic property.'

eighteen

T HE BREAKFAST was a simple affair of stale pastries, not enough tea bags and tinned fruit juice. Larry Fenton scarcely noticed. Of course Joanna was with him, but he was mostly preoccupied with his 'project', which now really did seem to be leading somewhere. They had arrived in Rome three days earlier, and had booked into the Albergo Cesare in the city centre.

Fenton was sure that, provided he kept well away from his apartment, it would still take a few more days for officialdom of any sort to find him. So he had booked into this hotel where he knew the owner well. The latter, although suggestively sceptical about the pretext put to him, agreed that Fenton would be registered under the name of Waley.

The hard yellow light of the early morning edged down the tops of the buildings around the Piazza Barberini. It would be another hour before the sun reached the fountain in the middle where, in 1640, Bernini left his statue of Triton to gargle a cascade forever. Leaving the Piazza, Fenton walked on downhill. The traffic was still light, and there were few pedestrians. It took him only ten minutes to reach the *Il Tempo* offices.

Toni arrived at 9 o'clock sharp and set about working on the third negative. Fenton was occupied with a mass of China reference material that he had assembled. He was browsing through it when, at 11 a.m., the telephone rang. A female voice asked to speak to Fenton.

'This is Dr Francesca Albani ... Signora Waley is in my surgery. She had a fall on some steps. Nothing serious, but she's quite shaken. Perhaps you could come round. The address is via Zuchelli 38, ground floor. It's not far—'

'Good God! Is ... is she—'

'Don't worry, Signor Fenton. Nothing bad. Will you

come?'

'Yes, of course. Thank you, I know the street. Let me speak to her, please.'

'Well, I am sorry, but the Signora is resting now; she is under slight sedation. So you will come round?'

'I'll be there in fifteen minutes!'

Shocked and concerned about Joanna, but also vexed by what was a minor disruption to the programme, Fenton recovered the negative from Toni, and told the Italian to break off for an hour.

Fenton stomped across the square outside the building, trying to suppress his slight feeling of annoyance. Falling over, for God's sake, at a time like this! She was only supposed to be shopping and sightseeing – nothing that should lead her to a doctor's surgery!

He had reached the edge of the square, waiting to cross the Via Del Corso – the main thoroughfare – when he heard his name called out. He turned to look, but someone brushed past and Fenton was startled to find an envelope thrust into his hands. He was looking down at that, rather than the bearer who was saying: 'I called you just now.'

He really didn't notice the features. All he saw was a youngish woman with a red scarf wrapped round the bottom of her face, hopping on the back of a waiting motorcycle, which immediately took off at high speed.

The unsealed envelope had the word 'urgent' scrawled on it with a felt pen. Fenton flicked open the flap. His first impression was that the Polaroid print was still fresh and sticky to the touch. Then he was staring, horrified, at a bust photograph of Joanna wearing the silk blouse she had bought the previous day, and chosen to wear this morning.

The face shocked him. It had the drawn, wide-eyed look of somebody petrified. The hands were not visible and there was no discernible background to the rough and ready portrait style print. Compounding the shock, even without the chilling signature at the bottom of the print, there was something in the pose that anybody then living in Italy would have recognised. Fenton had noted – with more or less dispassionate interest – many similar photographs in newspapers over the past few years. This time it had happened to him, and he was seized with a paralysing dread.

For a moment his head reeled and he felt sick. He stared again at the notorious logo: 'GAP' – rendered as usual in a studiedly infantile jumble.

Fenton looked round wildly in an absurd search for the bearer of the envelope. One or two passers-by stared at him. Then he saw that a few words were scribbled on the back of the envelope: *'Wait by your office telephone. Meanwhile, DON'T TALK.'*

In a pandemonium of car horns and screeching tyres, a murky orange single-decker bus belching black diesel fumes swerved violently to avoid Fenton as he ran across the road. He dived into a café where half a dozen people were gulping down a late counter breakfast, and they all turned to study Fenton as he collected a *gettone* at the cash-desk and rushed to a telephone stuck on the wall.

'Fenton ... er ... *Waley*! Did the Signora go out?' His voice was half choking in a dry throat.

'Yes, sir – not long after you called.' The hotel receptionist sounded mildly surprised. It was perhaps the odd mix-up of names.

'What? What call?'

'Well, it came from *Il Tempo* – I assumed it was from you, Signor. Do you want to leave a message? ... Hello...?'

But Fenton had dropped the receiver, and was already out the door and running back again towards the office. It was now clear that he could have used any name. He weaved in and out of the parked cars cluttering up the forecourt of the newspaper building.

At that hour, only a few of the press staff were around. He hurried through a ground floor corridor and then up the stairs past a series of empty offices. He pushed his head into the switchboard room where a girl in front of a PABX system, and with a nail file in her hand, jumped at the unexpected intrusion.

'Fenton – extension fifty-seven. Has there been any call

for me?'

'*Niente.*'

At a slower pace now, Fenton made his way towards his temporary working quarters, the deputy editor's office on the third floor. A cleaner playfully shoved a broom at him and muttered *buon giorno,* and one or two administrative or technical people nodded a greeting, but Fenton had never felt more alone, more isolated.

He subsided at his desk and stared again at the greyish, contrast-lacking 6 x 8 Polaroid print.

The first suffocating panic died away. 'Think Larry, *think...*' he said to himself. He started to weigh the options. The police, or more specifically the DIGOS,[*] had enjoyed some recent successes against the GAP. Fenton knew a DIGOS officer slightly. But the words 'Don't talk' leapt at him from the envelope.

Then there were his fellow journalists: alert the *Il Tempo* people – they could be trusted, and the editor was an old friend. The embassy, of course: Joanna was a British subject, after all – and a well known one. Was that a viable option? But... 'Don't talk.'

Anyway what were they *doing*, the GAP? Why should these Italian extreme left urban guerrillas kidnap a foreigner?

Apart from one or two obvious American military victims, until now GAP violence had been directed at Italian targets of the established order – judges, police, politicians, journalists, labour leaders ... What, in God's name, were they doing with Joanna of all people!

Steve Makins, one of the *Newsweek* people, or Foley of Reuters – they had both been in Italy a long time and would have some ideas. Fenton looked at the telephone. The two words 'Don't talk' had it over the rest.

In most kidnappings, people usually didn't talk, as the

---

[*] DIGOS – *Divisioni Investigazioni Generali e Operazioni Speciali* – Italian police anti-terrorist unit.

police bitterly complained. Thoughts such as these reeled around Fenton's head like a dog chasing its tail, until a gradual, deadening wave of resignation took over. His feelings of helplessness became bound up in fear. With no acceptable, safe option to explore, Fenton slumped into the chair at his desk, waiting by the telephone as instructed.

An awful feeling of guilt suddenly invaded him. Uninvited, he had crashed back into Joanna's life a few days ago. The fact that she was in Italy in the first place was his fault. It was all his fault.

In an onslaught of chaotic speculation, Fenton could see only one possible angle – and one especially painful for him: the targeting of Joanna had to be tied in some way to the Chinese bombshell document. That was his reluctant assumption. But how, suddenly, did these Italian terrorists, the GAP, even *know* about the film? He couldn't make any sense of it. God, how he hoped and prayed that nothing would happen—

Fenton jumped from the chair. The telephone was ringing. It had been many years since his legs were trembling like that.

*

The Via Del Corso strikes straight through the heart of the expensive, downtown part of the city. It's a long haul from the huge Vittoriano monument at one end to the spacious Piazza Del Populo spiked into place by an eighty-feet-tall Egyptian obelisk at the other. As the name suggests, the Corso was originally destined for games and races. Fenton simply walked. That is what he had been instructed to do, though he didn't know for how long.

A continuous conveyor belt of traffic moved down the line of banks, boutiques and picture galleries. A few minutes' excursion on either side of the Corso would take in a good number of Rome's well-known landmarks: the Pantheon, the Trevi fountain, the Piazza di Spagna and the fashionable shops huddled in the two acres of pedestrian-only side streets.

Fenton walked on, his eyes on every passer-by. He suddenly sensed that it was coming from behind, that somebody in the crowd was keeping pace with him. He stopped frequently and looked back, but all he saw was the irritation of those people he was obstructing.

Then the man was unexpectedly at his side. Fenton stared at him and, as if at journey's end, he halted abruptly.

'Keep walking. There's a café fifty metres down on the left.'

Mechanically Fenton went on. He was bewildered. The man beside him was like scores, hundreds, of others he had passed in the last half mile from the *Il Tempo* building. Mid-thirties, well-dressed in a light grey suit – he could have been a bank official, a high-class shop assistant, a lawyer, a civil servant – anything! He was wearing dark glasses, but that was true of half the Italian urban population.

They reached the café and sat down at an outside table. A waiter arrived in a flash. Fenton's escort ordered a coffee for himself, but Fenton shook his head, unable to speak.

'All right. You've already got the message ... This is the moment. Hand it over – the film – and we can move on.'

The Italian had one elbow on the table. He finished his cappuccino and lowered the cup delicately into the saucer. The other hand was ranging free and although it didn't look threatening, Fenton thought that it could quickly have a gun in it. Would he really brandish a gun in a public place like this? Anyway, it was scarcely the point.

Fenton pushed a small envelope across the table.

'But there's only one print in here, negative – or whatever!'

'It's the one we are working on in the office. I had no time—'

'Where's the rest?'

'At my apartment.'

A slight tightening of the muscles round the Italian's mouth said it all. If Fenton could have seen the eyes behind the sunglasses, the reaction would have been complete even without the slowly articulated comment: 'I don't believe you ... You are staying at the Albergo Cesare. You haven't been near your apartment since you arrived in Rome!'

'You mean I haven't been noticed,' said Fenton, willing up some reaction.

The Italian drove a finger round the dregs in his coffee cup. He held up this finger, either in a vulgar gesture, or as if to lick it. Finally he wiped it with a handkerchief.

'Look, Signor Fenton, we are in the middle of a transaction. We don't want complications. Easy we go and no problem, okay? You and I will now go to your apartment.'

The man stood up, gesturing with his head for Fenton to join him. They moved to the kerb, and a taxi pulled up almost instantly. Fenton had now got enough grip of himself to feel bitter even about that. He would sometimes spend thirty minutes or more tramping the streets looking for a taxi.

They took the narrow one-way Ponte Sisto across the Tevere, and then swung up between the Gianicolo hilltop gardens and another lush park, the Villa Schiarra, which was Fenton's favourite Sunday strolling ground.

For the whole journey Fenton said nothing to the man beside him. At first, the silence seemed called for on account of what would no doubt be a very intrigued driver. As they drove on, Fenton noticed that the driver spent an unnecessary amount of time looking in the rearview mirror. There was something else about him – or was it the car? The usual trappings were somehow too new, too insistent: the No Smoking notice, the photo of the family on the dashboard, the tariff sheet, a radio with an unaccounted for black box mounted under it and the plastic-sheeted advertisements stuck round the interior. It could have been a brand-new taxi. Fenton thought it was a taxi and a half ...

They pulled up at the apartment building, with Fenton half-expecting the *portiera* to amble out of her strategic bolthole as soon as he appeared. She was thankfully not around, although her presence wouldn't have made much difference. Fenton used his spare key, opened up the apartment and walked straight through to the salon, which was still half darkened by the closed shutters. The Italian followed a few steps behind. Fenton quickly fished out an envelope from one of the drawers in his desk and slipped it into his breast pocket. He then moved towards a tall cupboard by the door, uttering a string of vague comments as he went: 'That's it. It can't be … It makes no sense … I don't know what the hell you're doing… But let's get on with it. We can go.'

He was desperately hoping that the Italian would listen rather than watch. He pulled an old, lightweight raincoat from a hanger in the cupboard. It was something he had thought of during the taxi ride. The other man had his head cocked slightly to one side, and he was stroking his chin. The eyes were still hidden behind dark glasses worn even there, in the dim context of the shuttered apartment. He suddenly took a step towards Fenton.

'You can give me the film now – all of it! Believe me, if you're still fooling around, you will soon wish—'

'It's all here,' snapped Fenton, and he tapped his jacket pocket, 'but I'm keeping it until I see Signora Waley!'

The Italian sighed noisily and threw his hands in the air in a show of Latin exasperation.

'What a way to do business,' he said in a slow, sorrowful tone.

It had distracted Fenton. He scarcely saw the movement. The Italian had ducked, and with the agility of a Thai boxer, a foot swung round parallel to the floor. It was a lightning pass, which slammed painfully into Fenton's wrist.

The raincoat was wrenched off his arm and flung to the floor. It made a curious thud followed by a noise like the clatter of marbles spilled on parquet. Fenton stood there, stunned, and holding his wrist. He watched in amazement as the Italian bent down and started scooping up the score or more rounds of ammunition strewn on the floor.

'Pick it up, *cretino*! You can't leave that lying all over the place!'

In a slow, dreamlike manner, Fenton found himself stooping down to do his bit to recover the scattered rounds.

The Italian dropped a handful of bullets into one pocket of the raincoat and from the other pulled out a pistol, which he examined with professional interest. It was an old 1950 model ten-shot Beretta. Fenton had acquired the weapon illegally some years ago. He had never used it, except to try it out on a deserted beach while on holiday once in Sardinia. He kept it for unlikely emergencies, and there had been no such thing until today.

He had always thought that leaving the gun in the old coat was neat and inventive. Apparently the arrangement was not new. But it was the reason why Fenton had contrived to come to the apartment. He already had all the film tucked away in his jacket.

The Italian gave an amused, remonstrative cackle. He returned the gun to the pocket, bundled up the coat and threw it on a chair.

'You're a fool, Fenton … *il buffone del Tempo!* Playtime over. You give me the film now.'

'When I see Signora Waley. Not before.'

The Italian exploded his lungs impatiently. The fact that he had been told to expect it, was irrelevant. He turned towards the door muttering to himself. Fenton couldn't hear it all, but he understood something about having 'better things to do than waste a lot of time with a pig-headed *inglese*'.

If Fenton had any lingering doubts about the taxi, they were now dispelled. Downstairs the same car was waiting for them.

On any normal day, their presence would scarcely have registered with him; however, during this ride, Fenton's eyes fell on every kind of policeman. Whether they were on foot, on motorcycles or in cars, Fenton's gaze was drawn to them. They were especially thick on the ground as the taxi spun round the edge of St. Peter's square. He tried to suppress the ever-present and dubious hope that somebody in uniform would see fit to stop the yellow Fiat 1100. But the taxi went boring through the traffic like a fire engine.

They joined a line of vehicles snaking round a bend of the Tevere. It was all moving quickly and they were soon past the complex of sports stadia and the tall column that must be about the only monument in Rome that mentions *Il Duce* – Mussolini, for most. For some reason, there were an exceptional number of police cars around the turn-off for the Ministry of Foreign Affairs building on the left. Fenton swivelled in his seat to watch them being left behind.

Then they were going up the short curl of a service ramp onto a main route leading north. The taxi slowed and was overtaken by a small van. Both vehicles stopped on the ramp. The Italian nudged Fenton.

'Move yourself,' he said with no particular violence, 'this is our connection.'

He opened the rear doors of the van and gestured to Fenton to get in. He squatted down opposite Fenton on a side-mounted bench seat. The van drove off at a leisurely pace.

The only windows, at the top of the rear doors, were painted over. To Fenton, it felt as if he had been shut in a large cupboard. But the roof light was on – a sort of reminder not to mess around. For the first few minutes, Fenton tried to orientate himself by listening to the volume of traffic and guessing which major intersection they had reached. It must have been obvious what he was doing. His companion finally snatched a newspaper stuck behind a panel strut and tossed it to Fenton.

'Read this – it will keep your mind off things.' It was said so casually that he could have been delivering groceries.

A hot, claustrophobic twenty minutes passed. The newspaper remained folded on Fenton's knees. His mind was in a frantic turmoil again. The incident at the apartment had thrown him still further off balance. The measure of control that he had willed into his earlier reactions had now largely gone. It was the easy competence, the assurance of these people that so unnerved him. He felt caught up in a momentum of somebody else's making and in which he was being helplessly swept along. And there was something else: it changed nothing in his immediate plight, but the man escorting him didn't exactly fit with his idea of a GAP activist.

The van had slowed and was now almost crawling uphill. The bumping and the rasp and crackle of the tyres told Fenton that they were now on a rough track. Then the van stopped, the motor still running. After some seconds, the Italian leaned forward towards the driving cab. But he continued to face Fenton. He rapped on the panel and spoke into a tile-sized opaque grill behind the driver's seat.

'What have we got here?'

'Nothing ... Letting an old girl get away ... She's off, going down on her bike.'

The wheels raked at the rubble and the van lurched forward again. Another stop and Fenton heard what seemed to be the sliding door of a garage being opened. There were more bangs, movement, scuffling of feet and rattles. The Italian edged to the rear of the van, opened the doors and beckoned Fenton to get out.

A man dressed in a T-shirt and the bottom-half of a tracksuit was waiting. If his face had not been screwed up in distaste at the exhaust fumes, he would have looked bored. But he showed his muscles as he flapped his arms at the smoke.

Fenton tried, but he couldn't take it all in. They walked along a short, windowless corridor dimly lit by a single lamp in the cement ceiling, and reached a heavy wooden door with a metal grill at the top, which could have led to a cellar.

'No, not there. He's wanted upstairs.' Another man had just slipped in to join the party. He snapped out the comment and grabbed Fenton's arm.

They turned once, twice and then up some stone steps into another passage. Fenton gave up trying to remember. A door was pushed open. He baulked at seeing little of the dim interior, but was prodded forward. Then a light came on, revealing a small room in which the only furnishings were a cheap wooden table, a couple of chairs and a rolled-up mattress in a corner. Heavy jute curtains were drawn across two windows. Chinks of daylight still shone through the closed outside shutters.

'Well, this is the middle of the bridge,' said the original escort briskly, in what seemed to be a reference to the traditional point of exchange.

He moved in front of Fenton, who was still marshalled by the other man. The latter now had his arm firmly crooked round Fenton's neck.

The escort hoisted his rear onto the table. With one foot on the floor, the other was left dangling to and fro. It was a picture of relaxed insolence. Despite everything, it made Fenton bridle inwardly. Since 10.30 that morning, although he had been at the centre of violent crime – kidnapping, extortion and a one-sided athletic show-down at his apartment – no shots had been fired, no pistols or knives brandished. He hadn't seen a weapon of any sort except his own. And the irrelevance of *that* was demonstrated at once.

'We now check through the film.' The Italian's head moved slightly and the reflection of the single overhead light flashed briefly on his glasses. 'Then we can all go home,' he added.

'Where's Signora Waley? I do nothing until I see her!' It was said with determination and, given the chance, Fenton would have fought to prove his point. The grip round his neck had become so tight that he barely noticed the prick of a needle.

'Calm, let's have some calm! She is coming. All we need is—'

'No!'

'Listen, just take it easy ... Nobody getting hurt ... Got an agreement, you and me ... Relax ... All under control...'

There was more of the same for some seconds. But Fenton didn't hear it. He slumped to the floor.

nineteen

T HE VOICES were there tormenting Fenton in a wretched, nightmarish confusion. His mind was in continued replay. One moment it was registering scraps of familiar language, an instant later it would flash to fantasy – and then back again to some coherent sequence. Relief – of a kind – from the mental chaos eventually came from a sudden awareness of the tape stuck across his mouth. And with that came a first more-or-less lucid thought: he had been drugged in some way.

Little by little, the voices took on recognisable aspects. One man's English was largely smothered by a lot of insistent Italian from several other people. For several minutes, Fenton half listened to the babble in the next room while trying to recall what had happened to him. His last memory was of feeling faint and falling. After that, nothing...

Ideas came and went, but his head was swimming and it felt heavy to support. In fact, his whole body seemed weighed down and unresponsive, and the idea of nightmare came back to Fenton. Then he realised that he was bound to a chair.

In the near darkness, he could just make out the position of the door from a few cracks of light around the edges. There was something odd about that. The angles were wrong. He found that the chair to which he was strapped, had been raised up on a table. If the main purpose of this was to discourage rocking about, it was also an additional and humiliating reminder of his vulnerability.

The discussion in the next room became more obviously an argument. Fenton could hear the louder comments:

'I tell you it wasn't necessary.'

'I tell *you* something – your little game with Stefano was stupid and dangerous – that could have cost a few lives, so-called diplomats or not!'

'... business ... reasonable precaution ...'

'*Cretino* – imbecile!'

A third man joined in the exchange, but in a much softer voice that Fenton couldn't hear. Then the tone heightened again:

'You talk about "dangerous" – you should get your people out of here! There's no point in hanging around. It's over. We've recovered the film and you and Pasquali have been paid – you heard Stefano on the telephone confirming the transfers.'

'We wait until he gets here and tells me in person. How do I know he didn't have a gun to his head?'

'We don't operate like that.'

A raucous cry of derision broke in: 'Fine – but half an hour more will change nothing.'

'... So I want to talk to Fenton and the woman ...'

Fenton caught his breath. Thank God! 'The woman' – it had to be Joanna, he thought. It meant that she was unharmed, didn't it?

'Paolo!'

A man answered, apparently some distance away in another room.

'If it's under control, take the plaster off – but the chair stays on until I tell you. And you ...' the voice changed pitch, addressing somebody nearby, 'same thing for that *Il Tempo* rubbish in there!'

The door swung open and the sudden glare from the sunlit room seared through Fenton's eyes and sickening heaviness seemed to float around in the back of his skull. Then somebody was there, manhandling the chair off the table. The man's face was close to Fenton's ear.

'I take the gag off. If you start shouting, you'll be cracked on the head again. *Hai capito?*'

Fenton's head sagged a little in the way of nod. Another man arrived and the two of them carted Fenton out. His impression of this room was the same as before – that it was not regularly lived in. Something in the air, the light and the lack of noise from the open windows told him that they were well outside the city. His two handlers now had their backs to him watching the other door, and listening to some scrapes, thuds and soft swearing as somebody with a load came down the stairs.

Joanna was dumped against a wall. She was tied to a chair in the same way as Fenton. He didn't even think. The obvious but inadequate question was blurted out – he couldn't stop himself.

'Joanna! Are you all right?'

Joanna nodded. She looked pale but almost unnaturally calm. It was the sort of awful composure that comes to those exposed and then resigned to continuing terror.

'Get down there and watch for Stefano.' The voice, Italian, was clear and assured. Two men left immediately. Fenton's eyes turned to the one who had spoken.

Anywhere else, in the street, in a public place, he probably would have laughed. But now he stared, shocked, at the man in a fashionably cut dark suit and whose face was hidden by a child's party mask.

Then Fenton noticed the other man. It wasn't quite recognition – merely the vague feeling that he had seen this person before. At first glance, it was the general bearing and style that impressed; it took some moments before Fenton realised that it was a Chinese man sitting there. He seemed to be checking the labels on several liquor bottles set out with some beer cans and glasses on a small cloth-covered table.

With his mind battered by recent events, Fenton had difficulty in concentrating. At first, he couldn't even see anything unusual about this Chinese pouring a quarter of a bottle of Grappa over a handkerchief spread out in a large glass ashtray.

In Gerry Tan's hand, however, was an envelope, which Fenton did recognise. Tan shook the negatives onto the handkerchief. A pass of his other hand, and a silver lighter gleamed. Then with a soft 'whoosh' there was an immediate conflagration a foot high. The yellow flames had a sooty

edging, and the acrid smell of burning celluloid was
noticeable at once. Tan stepped back, watching the blaze.
Then he looked over his shoulder at Fenton.

'There ... Chairman Mao can now rest in peace. And if
that ...' Tan gestured at the flames '... makes you feel
aggrieved, Mr Fenton, I should point out that you had no
right to the film in the first place.'

'Who the hell are you to talk about rights?' Fenton
retorted, in sudden anger. He started up, complete with the
chair, but was pulled back abruptly by the Italian. A loud
crack announced that one of the legs had snapped. Fenton
now had to struggle to keep the chair from toppling over.

'*Rights?*' he gasped furiously. 'I'm a journalist – I have
a duty—'

'Now is not the moment,' Tan broke in coolly, 'but we
might discuss that later.'

'*Perdio*, that's crazy!' The Italian was standing behind
Fenton. His mask was fixed on the small blaze.

'All that operation for ... for a piece of smoke?'

He shot his sleeve to look at his watch – flat, expensive,
no doubt very reliable, and in keeping with his general
elegance.

'I hold some people once ... We get a Canaletto. Then
some misunderstanding happens, flames everywhere, half
the house alight. Two people die trying to save the picture
from the fire. Then it turns out to be a fake.'

Suddenly they all looked up at the sound of busy
movement and voices in the forecourt. The Italian walked
over to a window. His head was still turned towards the
company, but at the same time he was trying to listen to a
conversation somewhere below. He lost patience.

'Okay, okay, Stefano – never mind all that,' he shouted,
'*Si o no?*'

'*Si, si!*'

They all heard that. The Italian jerked his head round
and fingered the mask. He seemed to be staring at each of
the others in turn. It wasn't clear whether he was
considering an appropriate farewell or an addition to his

Canaletto story. In the event, he said nothing at all. Instead, he made an eloquent gesture with his hand towards Tan, as if he were an MC offering the floor to the next performer. Then he slipped away, followed by his troops.

Doors slammed. Then a vehicle started up. That particular noise somehow brought to Fenton, still suffering and confused, a sudden shot of relief, of hope. He thought that it was the same van that had brought him to the villa.

Tan stood motionless by a window, watching the departure. He cried out something in Chinese; it seemed an unusually loud noise for him. Fenton assumed that it was a remark directed at the Italians.

Tan turned abruptly and moved towards Joanna. It was a moment to remember. He had a slim-bladed boning knife in his hand.

Joanna made a slight noise as her breath caught in her throat. Fenton stared, incredulous. It was grotesque – the small silver cufflinks, the expensive light-blue poplin shirt, distinguished tie and then that evil-looking slither blade.

There was no ripping or tearing – only a few sharp cracks as the knife sliced through the bindings. They had used the same kind of upholstery tape on them both.

He had made no noise at all, the other Chinese to whom Tan had actually called out. He could have dropped from the ceiling or come in from a window; but suddenly he was there. And he was the sort of Chinese Fenton could readily recognise: the short brush-cut hair left the other features more pronounced – the bland, flat face and small wedge-eyes. For the rest, it was the common short-sleeved white shirt, dark slacks and those soft moccasin slippers with a V-slit along the uppers that the comrades wear for anything from acrobatics to correctional periods of thought-study. He was gathering up the severed pieces of tape around the chair. Joanna crumpled forward with her head in her hands.

Then Fenton felt a sudden release on his own limbs as the bindings were cut. The Chinese moved over and bent down at the side of the chair. Fenton noticed that the muscled forearms belonged to a correspondingly solid torso.

He had a sudden vision of the man doing somersaults to the end of the room and then producing a very long piece of reconstituted upholstery tape.

'You have been put to a great deal of trouble, Mr Fenton.' Tan was saying conversationally.

Fenton gazed fixedly ahead of him. He was speechless. It couldn't be real.

Joanna looked up, open-mouthed and rubbing her wrists. Fenton got to his feet and the crippled chair fell over. He staggered for an instant and then went over to Joanna. He crouched down in front of her and put his hands on her knees. He was talking to her softly and he barely heard Tan.

'Your ... that is, Mrs Waley, has suffered a great deal, too. It is, to say the least, most regrettable that we were forced to use ... let's say ... forcible negotiation. You will find that you have been obliged to accept an agreeable outcome. More money than any number of articles would have been worth. You may not fully appreciate what I am saying ...'

Tan was by the host's table on which the cloth was now flecked with small particles of soot. He wiped a glass and then his hand hovered over the surprising cluster of bottles on the table. He shot a slight smile at Fenton.

'No Black Label, apparently.'

With a little shake of the head he settled for a new bottle of Dimple Haig and poured a generous dose into the glass.

'It will more than compensate—'

He stopped as Fenton stood up in a shaky, violent movement.

'I've gone through that already – the bribes, being paid off,' he raged, 'if I was to be bought off, it would have happened long before this!'

'Quite so,' said Tan, unruffled, 'But this is *after* the event. And now, essentially, you have nothing to be bought...'

It was a calm or silky observation, depending on your frame of mind.

'I think you should have a drink and consider the

reality, the practical aspects.' He held out the glass towards Fenton who ignored it.

'An innocent man, Jack Harper, was murdered because he was mistaken for me,' he shouted. 'And it's you, if I've got it right, who wanted me out of the way! I don't know who you are, and I don't much care – but don't for Christ's sake offer me money!'

Tan stared intently at Fenton. He took a sip from the glass that Fenton had declined to accept. The Chinese assistant was standing by the door, relaxed, impassive and probably understanding nothing of the conversation.

'You're right, of course,' Tan said slowly. 'But whether you believe it or not, I am telling you that it was a blunder, a tragic blunder.'

'Larry, I'm going to move over there ...' Joanna was pointing to the table. 'Yes, over there, and I'm going to get drinks.'

She spoke deliberately, but for some seconds she had difficulty in getting to her feet. Oddly, she pushed Fenton's offered hand away. She tottered a little and then kicked off her low-heeled sandals. She walked slowly towards the table.

Fenton watched, amazed, as Tan gestured vaguely at some of the bottles in the way of a solicitous host. Joanna hesitated.

'Larry?'

'Half a tumbler. Neat.'

Joanna busied herself with dispensing. At the same time, Fenton noticed that she seemed to be much steadier and that her right foot was creeping inch by inch along the wooden floor towards a small black stain. Then her toes closed over the mark and she bent down to rub her ankle.

Fenton had seen what it was finally. One of the negatives had fallen from the envelope, and had not gone up in Tan's ashtray incineration. The Chinese was saying quietly that they had the time to talk things over. But Fenton was looking at Joanna. Her drawn smile was too faint for nuances.

She had a glass in each hand. One, trembling slightly, was outstretched towards Fenton. It was from this hand that suddenly the glass jumped and smashed on the parquet.

*

There were several shots in quick succession from very close to the villa. Tan was already at one window and his nimble assistant at the other, peering at the fracas outside. Some shouting fifty yards away was cut off by more firing – two short bursts from an automatic weapon. A car somewhere, was revving violently in a low gear, as if it was slip-sliding up a steep bank. Inside the building, the Chinese were frantically trying to close all the metal screens. Tan yelled something at his colleague, who then darted from the room.

There were scurrying steps below, then thumps and some short, savage cries. The downstairs door cracked back on its hinges. A brief high-pitched shriek fell away into a terrible moan. A single shot crashed round the building, but the moaning went on.

Fenton huddled against Joanna, cradling her into a corner of the room. Tan stayed by a window where he had managed to close only one of the screens. He wheeled round as they came charging into the room. Joanna clung more tightly to Fenton.

It was a moment of paralysing panic. Tan, his teeth bared, had frozen into the window-frame. The earlier absence of weapons had struck Fenton; he wished it had stayed that way. Two of the Italians had machine pistols, and the one called Stefano had recovered his gun – through some odd Chinese courtesy at the Embassy, or more likely, simply acquired another.

'My God ...' Fenton muttered. He was terrified and he could feel Joanna's whole body shaking in his arms.

He saw immediately that one of the arrivals was the English-speaking boss of the party, without his mask. He turned out to be a darkly good-looking man of about thirty-five; but he had a livid purple birthmark on the left cheek and jaw. Apparently it no longer mattered.

'What the devil are you doing?' cried Tan. He had prised himself out of the woodwork. He stood quite still and erect.

The boss fanned his machine pistol around, and with his free hand he pointed at Tan.

'A Carabinieri patrol car blocked us in – and it's not just bad luck. We turned round and there was another which tried to ram us!'

'Why come here?' Tan hissed furiously. He hadn't moved, and the tension in his face muscles seemed to have squeezed all the colour out.

'I tell you, you clever little *bastardo* – there was no other route out of here! This must be your doing – or maybe the journalist talked.' He swung the pistol around at Fenton and Joanna, still huddled together in the corner.

Fenton couldn't move or speak. He stared, appalled, at the weapon five yards away, lined up to cut him and Joanna in half.

'But the firing – you're mad!'

'We're out of here *now* – and you three are coming with us!' he said, ignoring the outburst. 'You got us in here – you're getting us out. On the floor against the wall over there – move! Stefano, put the woman near the window.'

Car doors slammed not far from the house. Among a confusion of shouts, somebody was barking formal orders. Further away, there was the high-pitched wail of an ambulance siren. That could be heard at any time of the day, except as Fenton knew, they were well out of the city. The boss and the third man, Paolo, were stationed at the window corners watching the forecourt.

'If those two get any nearer, shoot them off it – we need that van!'

A second's silence and then:

'*Stronzo*! That's it ...'

It was deafening. Long after the short burst of fire, the room still seemed to be echoing with the noise. Joanna had buried her head against Fenton's chest. Then she was pulled away, with Stefano's eloquent pistol describing where she should go.

Fenton was mute and in thrall to fear, but some part of his mind was marvelling in an abstract, detached way at the effectiveness of the violence.

Paolo, the thirty-year-old average Italian well-dressed male who had rounded up Fenton, was now flicking his free hand over Tan's body in a search for weapons. He found none. Fenton was somehow relieved that the fish-skinning knife, or whatever it was, seemed to have disappeared. The boss made known his plans:

'I tell you now – no argument, no negotiation, we move immediately.'

The tone was controlled and cold. The dark eyes, hard and contemptuous, ranged over the three non-Italians.

'It won't be long and they have an assault gang outside – if it's not there already. So we move very quick. Somebody not doing how I say and I shoot, I lose nothing, okay?' He had a finger to the side of his face, indicating the birthmark.

What did that mean? An astonishing but crude psychological explanation flashed through Fenton's mind. Then he thought that the Italian simply meant that he was impossibly well-known – a marked man in another sense.

The boss turned and flicked his hand at Paolo. 'Go down and bring up the other Chinese.'

Joanna was half-slumped against the wall by a window. She was sobbing quietly with her hands over her face.

'Larry, I can't ... I think I'm going to ...'

'Slap that down quick.'

The boss had hardly snapped out the words when Stefano whipped his palm across Joanna's face. She gasped, looked up wildly but then fell silent. Fenton had flinched and jerked forward with an involuntary cry. A machine pistol was levelled at him, and he subsided again.

Paolo arrived at the doorway. Panting with the effort of the climb, he dragged the limp body into the room. The

Chinese was dead.

The boss stood behind a window and using the short barrel of his weapon he slowly edged open the one metal screen that Tan had got to earlier. In the forecourt, lay the two other Chinese, where they had been mown down.

'We've got four people in here!' It was a ringing shout.

The Italian waited. The faint noise of a high-flying jet only seemed to emphasise the sudden quiet outside the villa. Fenton wondered why the man had declared four people. The body of the Chinese on the floor could hardly count. The boss nodded to Stefano.

'One woman – English,' he called out. Stefano prodded Joanna to stand in the window frame. After a few seconds he pulled her away.

'You hear me?' yelled the boss. A moment's hesitation and then a voice answered from below, some twenty or thirty yards away.

'We're listening.'

'Two Chinese diplomats, English journalist and the woman ... We are moving out with them. No discussion, no talk – you do as I say or we drop them one at a time.'

'I am calling on you to lay down your weapons and surrender. The villa is surrounded and—'

The formal demand common to most forces of law and order was interrupted by the boss:

'Get somebody – hands in the air – to the van and have him back it up to the porch; rear doors open and engine running!'

Again there was a pause before the same man answered.

'I have no authority to do that. Somebody from headquarters will have to—'

'*Cretino!* Over there ... You, you can give orders. I can see your insignia, *Colonello* – just do what I say.'

'Cool it and wait.'

The boss wheeled round and took two steps towards the body of the slain Chinese. He fired two rounds into the parquet. Bouquets of splintered wood erupted from the floor. Then he and Stefano bundled the body to the window.

There they humped the form onto the ledge and pushed it over to join the others outside. That Chinese did count after all.

The immediate thud and splatter of gravel was followed by a raucous cry from below:

'*Calma, calma*! Stop it all. We'll move the van.' The voice was that of the Colonel, and it had a metallic echo from the loud-hailer.

'Bring it up *now*, or we'll drop the next one.' The boss peered round the screen with infinite caution. Something was happening below.

He wore a helmet, which gave some protection to his head and face, and he was weighed down by a bullet-proof vest, but it was a brave man, holding his hands half-raised, who walked across the middle of the forecourt to where the van was stationed.

They heard the starter thrash round in two unproductive bursts. The motor responded at the third attempt.

Fenton was breathing deeply and irregularly as he struggled to control the erratic clumping of his heart. Joanna had crumpled against the wall, unable to stand; her face was white, immobile, as if in a trance. Only the Chinese, Tan, seemed in control, arms folded, watching ...

As Paolo dragged Joanna to her feet, and then marshalled all three hostages towards the door, the boss slammed open the metal screen across the window:

'We're coming down to the van. Don't try clever stuff. Anything I don't like down there, we shoot again – the woman first!'

Tan's eyes darted to Joanna and Fenton. His lips were thin, over his well-tended teeth, and tightened into a bitter smile. It was about the only sign of emotion he had shown. He looked more frustrated and angry than frightened.

'This is when hostage-taking looks—'

He got no further. A savage blow to the side of his face from the butt of an automatic brought blood flowing from his mouth and nose, and his glasses spun off. The boss prodded Tan's stomach with the machine pistol.

'You ...' he rasped. 'If you're still alive, we are going to have some talks – just you and me when—'

He didn't finish the sentence. A brilliant flash of white enveloped everything. The blinding was immediate and complete. A dull, heavy explosion seemed to lift the floor. Fenton and Joanna were flung flat. Instantly they could smell it – dense, billowing smoke, which filled the room. People were screaming everywhere because of the intense pain in the ears. The room seemed to have become a huge reverberating kettledrum. The pain pulsed with the flexing walls and trampoline floor.

When it came, the harsh crackle of automatic fire seemed remote, almost comforting – something recognisable. It lasted only a few seconds.

Fenton became aware of movement, of hunched agile forms with huge space-age earmuffs. He heard thin, tinny shouts through his partial deafness. Over and over again the order was repeated: '*Non muovetevi!*'

Some more vision returned and Fenton vaguely saw Joanna staggering about with both hands outstretched as if hoping they would find the door for her. Fenton lurched forward to restrain her. She had not understood the order not to move. He was stumbling, treading on air.

It seemed to come from a long way away, a single report. Fenton spun round with the shock and then fell. A random shot had torn into his shoulder. It scarcely hurt at all – more a violent ripping of his jacket sleeve. All his pain sensors seemed to be occupied with the frightful assault on his ears. Two more isolated shots were fired somewhere and then it seemed to be over. The smoke still hung around, but now was clearing slowly.

He was curled up on the floor among the flakes of plaster debris from the ceiling and walls, aware of people moving around him. His eyes were closed and his hearing had become something else – it was more the vibration of feet on the parquet that he sensed. Then somebody was bending over him. He was propped up in stages.

'Joanna ... the Signora ...' The mumbled words echoed

in his head as if his ears were tightly blocked.

'Okay, okay. She's all right. No problem. Already outside.'

The face mouthing these faint words belonged to an unknown Italian with a shoe-brush moustache and wearing dark combat gear. He was beaming assurance from about a foot away.

Fenton was pulled gently to his feet and he let himself be led towards the door. His legs seemed to be pedalling in space. He had lost all sense of balance and he had to be supported on both sides. After a few paces he felt his mind slipping away. Then he recognised Tan emerging from the door, and being helped down the stairs. It was a laborious operation, one step at a time, but the man was technically mobile.

The sight of this particular Chinese still upright had some kind of stiffening effect on Fenton. In the manner of a stubborn, conscious drunk, he made extra, deliberate efforts.

Another man in battle fatigues brushed past them and raced up the stairs. He had some dark grey blankets over his arm.

Somehow Fenton kept going until they were out of the villa building and into the courtyard. He looked at a knot of people standing round a heap on the ground – it was immediately under one of the upper windows. There was already a blanket over that heap. Then, to his huge relief, Fenton had a glimpse of Joanna sitting half into the open door of one of the police vans. He thought that he had cried out a word of comfort. That was the last thing he remembered, although they told him afterwards that he had walked to the ambulance.

twenty

A NIGHT HAD PASSED. Larry Fenton had spent most of it in a not unpleasant half-waking, twilight state. He knew that they had treated and stitched his punctured shoulder, using a local anaesthetic. Other injections had left him drowsy, but partially aware of events. Hour by hour, his hearing gradually returned to normal. The acute suffering in the ears softened to a dull ache by early morning, and it was the tightness and increasingly felt pain in the strapped-up shoulder that now bothered him more.

After the events of the last few weeks, the medical aftermath was proving strangely run-of-the-mill. The doctors, demonstrably competent, were casually amiable in manner, as were the nurses in this clinic staffed by nuns. Fenton felt surprised, and even a little aggrieved, that he was being treated as if he had been the victim of any mundane accident. The only concession, apparently, to his exceptional recent history, was that they had put him in a private room. Fenton wondered who was paying for it.

The drugs had left him relaxed and calm mentally. He had also been greatly relieved when they were able to tell him that Joanna, shocked more than harmed was resting in the same clinic, and that she would be around to see him in due course.

A friendly nurse provided him with a transistor radio. None of the news broadcasts made any mention of the assault on the villa – despite what had been a huge fracas involving an exotic mixture of Italian gangsters and, so it seemed, some kind of Chinese diplomats. Moreover, the rescue was an impressively-staged operation; whenever the British SAS did things like that, the media were on about it for weeks. Fenton didn't know what to make of it.

Half way through the morning he felt well enough to

call the *Il Tempo* editor at his home. But from the moment when he was connected on the bedside extension, he knew that something indeed had happened to his overall story – and to the spectacular 'villa' finale. *'Drammatico...'* the editor warmly conceded; but for all that, Fenton had the impression that the affair was being treated simply as an unfortunate, commonplace incident.

Fenton wondered if, after all, the blast had affected his brain. Everything seemed false, unreal. He was incredulous, baffled by the composed 'take your time' and 'we'll see you later' reaction. The editor was manifestly aware of all that had happened but his main interest, gratifying in a sense, was in Fenton's and Joanna's well-being. Fenton's big story seemed almost nonexistent – secondary and smothered in an Italian torrent of concern about injuries and convalescence.

A nun-nurse came to the doorway and caught Fenton inspecting his face in a shaving mirror. He was shaking his head in disbelief, but the despairing look of incomprehension suddenly changed to a smile.

'A visitor for you.'

Fenton put down the mirror on the bedside locker and smiled. This would be Joanna.

There was a clattering of something on the highly polished stone floor outside. A man's voice apologised in English. The nurse held the door open with one hand, and with the other, passed the fallen walking stick to its owner.

'Good morning,' Marriot said, carefully closing the door behind him.

He cut an elegant figure with his trim white hair, Hong Kong tan and well-made beige linen suit. The material fell straight down one leg, but the limp was less obvious than might be expected. Using the hook of his stick he manoeuvred, with habitual ease, a white-painted chair nearer the bed. He left the stick hanging on the back of his chair and sat down. Both hands seized his prosthetic leg and hauled it across onto the other, good knee.

'You've had a rough time,' he said. He stared at Fenton with that look of steady appraisal found in consulting rooms and police stations.

'Just what the hell are you doing here?' Fenton felt a hard cuff of disappointment that the visitor was not Joanna. To be confronted instead by Marriot added insult to injury.

'Well, let's say that somebody is looking after the interests of British subjects in trouble.'

'Christ – what hogwash!' Fenton really wanted to unleash a whole tirade of abuse, but he wasn't all that sure of his ground. He said nothing more. Tightly closed lips rolled inwards against the teeth left him looking obviously angry and defiant.

Marriot ignored the outburst and went on in his quiet, persuasive way. 'There will be some technical people coming to see you later. I hope you will cooperate. They will want to know, as accurately as possible, the effects ... well, how the ... er ... how the blast affected you.'

'Yes, what in God's name was it – that frightful explosion!'

'Well, that's not strictly my field. Enough to say that it was an ADD, or aural-directed device – you know, the ears ... No doubt you noticed.'

Fenton raised his eyes to the ceiling.

'I mean,' Marriot went on, 'apart from the temporary blinding and all the smoke and fireworks, some advanced low-frequency technology was involved. As a matter of fact, it hasn't been used before—'

'What! You mean ... you bastards! You mean you used us as guinea pigs?'

For a moment Fenton's nostrils were flaring and his cheeks pinched white with fury.

'There has to be a first time. And, after all, apart from those who were already dead, you all got out of there, didn't you?' Marriot frowned like a vexed schoolmaster.

Fenton regained control of himself, but for seconds he was speechless. He sensed even more that the affair, in a calculated way, was being reduced to a humdrum incident in which he, Larry Fenton, just happened to be involved. He couldn't articulate his outrage and frustration. He sought refuge in a humdrum question.

'Now you tell me, Marriot, you owe me this – how was the operation organised so quickly? How did you even know that I was in Rome? How can you—'

Marriot put up his hand to deflect further questions.

'The simple answer,' he said with a slight smile, 'is that there was unusual conduct of the target, as we say. In this case, there were several targets – all leading us to the same place. It may even amuse you to know that yesterday morning a car hired by the Soviet Embassy was involved in a crash less than a mile from the villa. Nobody was killed or seriously hurt, but they gave up and ... and they all went home.'

Fenton thought about that and mulled over possible identities for the other so-called targets. Marriot went on in the same mundane, practical vein:

'Yes, the Chinese. What did you think of him? He's the one we're really interested in.'

'What about him?' said Fenton stiffly. His face was set in a tight, defensive expression.

'General behaviour, how he came across to you ...'

It was a mark of Marriot's skill as an interviewer, not to say interrogator, that he coaxed out of Fenton all that he could remember of the encounter. As the discussion developed, Fenton cursed himself for letting the other man lead him on. He was well aware that people in general, despite themselves, are anxious to impart acquired knowledge. And journalists, for obvious reasons, are even more prone to this than others. It was only late in the conversation that he bridled. For a time he had forgotten his priorities.

'But what the devil do you want my view for? You've got the little bastard to plug into the mains or whatever you do! What more do you want?'

Marriot's face screwed up into a grimace. He humped his chair an inch or two nearer the bed.

'Chinese Embassy people were there. They had a doctor – they intervened immediately. He went off with them.'

'What! Fenton yelled. He jerked forward in the bed. 'I don't believe you. The police, the Carabinieri ... The man's a crook, a kidnapper – he takes hostages ...' Fenton winced with pain; the sudden movement pulled at his damaged shoulder, and the shouting was hurting his ears.

Marriot was nodding sympathetically. He waited until Fenton calmed.

'You probably know, of course, that Italy is about to sign a multi-billion dollar contract with Peking for several oil explorations projects in China. The Italians are fairly well satisfied. They got three of their most wanted criminals – two dead ... the third will probably survive. They are still looking for another with GAP connections – and then there are all those links, precisely, with the GAP to follow up.'

'Well, who is he?'

'Who?'

'The Chinese guy – God, Marriot, you make me mad!'

'As a matter of fact, we're not absolutely sure.'

There was silence for a second or two. Fenton indulged in a forced, wolfish grin of derision, which Marriot dismissed with a flick of his hand.

'Oh yes, he's got a name of course, a nice address and an even nicer place of work – but that's not what I was talking about. Forget it ... Now then ...' Marriot edged the chair a little closer. 'The other thing I wanted to ask about was your plans – your writing plans, to be more precise. What do you have in mind?'

'Ah ...' Fenton eased back in the bed and pulled his injured shoulder into a more comfortable position. He liked the sound of that question at least. He stretched out his functioning arm towards the water jug. Marriot got to it first without having to move from the chair, and filled a glass.

'Thank you. I haven't had time to make up my mind yet. Why – what does that have to do with you?'

Fenton understood perfectly well of course the thrust of Marriot's question.

'You must be aware, of course, that it is desirable that you say nothing. Nothing at all. Assuming you disregard this advice, I suppose that you would have enough for a one-time "I-was-there" type of article.'

Marriot pursed his lips and nodded his head slightly as if weighing up and then reaffirming the estimate.

'What the hell do you mean?'

'I mean that's all you've got to sell, isn't it? An account, no doubt colourful, of a week's rough experience. But you can't publish a document that no longer exists!'

'Christ!' Fenton exclaimed. He coughed out a short laugh. 'Do you know, Marriot, in the space of little more than a week, people have been popping up all over the place trying to buy something and now everybody is rushing around telling me I've got nothing to sell!'

Marriot was nodding his head again in his sympathetic way.

'And anyway,' Fenton continued, 'how do you know that it no longer exists?'

'Ah, I talked to Mrs Waley before coming to see you. She explained how the Chinese destroyed the negatives.'

'I've seen and heard enough during the last week, believe me, to file some pretty good copy!' Fenton said, tapping the side of his head.

'Oh, I do believe you, Mr Fenton,' said Marriot equably. 'The point really is that, without the actual document, anything you now do is happily reduced from a potential disaster to ... to what? Perhaps a bit of embarrassment, I suppose. Still, give me a realistic figure of what you might earn from it. We'll double that plus ...' he paused and gestured with his hands round the room '... all this, expenses and so on.'

Fenton lurched forward in real anger. He was brought up suddenly by the pain of tearing stitches in his shoulder. He lay back, panting.

'You're an arrogant bastard, Marriot.' He knew that he was raging more against the system than the person. But he charged on: *'Bit of embarrassment?* It wasn't *you* – nearly killed, held hostage, shot and probably going to be half deaf for the rest of your life! Not you, Marriot. But you come here with a smile, and your suave touch trying to pay me off. It was your harassment, your interference – God, you've got a bloody nerve! And what about Jack Harper? That was supposed to be *me* murdered in Hong Kong!'

Fenton was gasping both with fury and the pain in his ears, which was becoming more acute with the shouting. And a thought was pawing at the back of his mind that he had made the point badly, if at all.

The other man didn't seem to think much of it either. He heaved himself out of the chair.

'Try to avoid naming names – that will help,' he said mildly.

As Marriot limped towards the door, Fenton suddenly realised that he had been raving on to a Security Service officer who'd had his leg blown off by a bomb or something – oh, God that was bad!

'Marriot ...?'

The MI5 man turned, leaning on his stick. Fenton hesitated, and then gave up. He flapped his hand in dismissal. Marriot nodded again and went out, closing the door quietly.

He had lost his leg in a car accident. But there was no reason why Fenton should have known that.

twenty-one

THE WINDOWS of the apartment were wide open. A half pulled Venetian blind, rustling occasionally in the soft breeze, deflected most of the afternoon glare. It was a quiet time of the day – really the siesta hour for most people, although this didn't mean much for Larry Fenton.

He was sitting at his long desk set immediately against the windows. He had filled a score of foolscap pages with his small, neat handwriting. Normally he would have run off the notes on a typewriter, but he found that when he tried, the hand action dragged too much at his shoulder.

Three days had passed since his return from the clinic. Joanna had already gone back to London. She had put on a brave face, but after one night together at the apartment, it was clear that she was still in a brittle state. She was hard-headed enough, however, not to let Fenton accompany her as he had wanted to do. 'Darling man,' she insisted, 'There's lots of time for us – and you have a job to finish.'

Fenton was indeed determined to finish something, although he was far from sure what final form it would take. He no longer had the key documentary evidence. What did he have? A mass of disorganised notes, British officialdom (and American, too, no doubt) in the form of Marriot frowning over his shoulder, a now apparently unhurried Italian editor and some extraordinary experience to relate.

He had just scratched through the word 'bomb' in favour of 'device' when the doorbell rang. He walked down the passageway with his text in his mind rather than anything else. Having lived through a period of sustained uncertainty and danger, Fenton had lapsed into a state of almost unnatural relaxation; his receptiveness to surprise was numbed.

He pulled open the door and stared with no particular emotion at the slender, trim, silver-haired Chinese. He was wearing a dark grey formal suit and he carried a briefcase. He would easily have passed for the diplomat the Italian thug had claimed him to be when shouting demands at the police. And nobody would have guessed that the plaster on his cheek covered a four-inch slit from the impact of the butt of a machine pistol.

'It is in your interest that we talk for a few minutes. May I come in?'

Fenton barely hesitated. He gave a cursory nod and stepped to one side to let the other man pass.

In the living room, Fenton gestured to the Chinese to sit down in one of the easy chairs at one end of the desk. He quickly gathered up his notes and put them to one side, face down. He would have done this confronted by any visitor.

'We didn't finish our earlier conversation, Mr Fenton,' said Gerry Tan mildly.

He made it sound as if there had been some trivial interruption. Fenton didn't react. He had become inured to what seemed to be a general complicity to downgrade the affair to somebody else's bad dream.

'Just who the hell *are* you?' Fenton said as he sat down. He folded his arms gingerly and tried resting his elbows on the desk. It proved uncomfortable and he leaned back in the chair with a sigh of impatience.

'I am the unfortunate who was responsible for recovering and destroying the document. That's done.'

Fenton gave a weary, dismissive wave with his good arm. But he watched very carefully as Tan opened the briefcase and placed a quarto Manila envelope on the desk.

'Twenty thousand US dollars. It's not a bribe – more

what I prefer to call due compensation. And of course, if you decide to write nothing, it should cover any lost earnings, or it will anyway help ...'

Fenton's breathing quickened. He had no doubt that the money was there. A judgement had to be made. He found that he couldn't do it right away.

'They are good, authentic US Treasury notes. Take a look ...' Tan was smiling wryly as he remembered how half this 'bonus' had been refused in style by the Italians.

'What's to stop me taking the money and then publishing my account anyway?' Fenton said tersely.

'Nothing. But really, Mr Fenton, what would be the point? You are not trying to expose something, prove a case or even rally the people. It would simply be a piece of journalistic self-indulgence. And you would always be looking over your shoulder.'

'That's a threat!' exclaimed Fenton with some eagerness. It was an idea to which he could react with some conviction.

'Let's just say that I just don't think you would find it worthwhile.' Tan closed his briefcase. He looked poised to leave, and nodded towards the packet.

'Take it. Not a fortune these days, but it's a considerable sum of money. So, first a holiday? Well, perhaps not Hong Kong ...'

'Leave all that. Here's a nice little detail.' Fenton was fingering through the pages of a small pocket-book. He found what he was looking for. He then looked up at Tan with deliberate calm – the prosecuting counsel about to pounce.

'I asked who you are. There's more to the question than you imagined, no doubt.' He closed the covers of the notebook, but left a finger between the pages. 'You say you were charged with destroying the document, the film.'

'That's right,' said the Chinese quietly. His eyes were fixed on Fenton.

'I don't believe you destroyed the film at all!'

The only sound came from the light scratch and clatter of the blind in the wind. For some seconds Tan's face betrayed nothing other than rigid attention. His worst fears were now confirmed. He had always assumed that there was a chance that Fenton would not be taken in by the small incineration charade. Moreover, the Mafioso, in a gratuitous and perverse aside about the fake Canaletto going up in smoke, could only have sharpened any existing doubts.

'That's a very odd remark, Mr Fenton.' He frowned and sounded perplexed. 'You and Mrs Waley – and one of the Italian crooks, for that matter – saw me burn it. Or perhaps you have forgotten?'

'You burnt a heap of substitute negatives of which this was one.'

Fenton opened the pocket-book and pushed a small scrap of dark celluloid across the desk.

'It fell on the floor at the villa. Joanna grabbed it seconds before the blast. Oh, there's Chinese print on it all right – but its part of a newspaper article about pig rearing in Southern China! I checked ...'

That was something Tan didn't expect, although it didn't change much in his overall reckoning. The look of concentration slowly faded from his face. He gave a short, tolerant laugh.

'Well, I personally don't know. But the most likely explanation is that it was dropped by one of the embassy staff who were around there. It's not unusual to have all kinds of material on film.'

'Exactly,' said Fenton with obviously insincere agreement, 'I knew it would be something like that. Just an idea that came to me.'

Tan stood up. He remained silent and still for a moment. His mind was racing. He began to edge towards the door in the manner of a visitor anxious to leave, but not quite knowing how to say goodbye. Fenton, sure that he had made a good, if reckless point, shuffled round from behind the desk, smiling grimly.

Gerry Tan walked slowly across the room towards the hallway with Fenton a pace behind. Thoughts flashed through his head: he had killed one man – a good man, ruthlessly sacrificed to protect his position. The certain fate awaiting Lee of torture and execution did nothing to relieve Tan's real remorse. And then there was Jack Harper. The Australian had violently resisted; the killing was a stupid, excessive act by a subordinate detailed to work for him, but who usually answered to another unit. That said, responsibility ultimately fell on him. It *all* fell on him.

For more than ten years in Hong Kong, he had kept Taiwan informed of everything he learned from being the improbable confidant, the undetected eyes and ears, at the highest level, of Peking (or of 'Beijing', rather, as he of course would say it when in Chinese company) .

The fine irony was that he was considered irreplaceable by both camps. He knew that sooner or later, in one way or another, Fenton would go public with the clever guess that the film was still in existence. Even the *suspicion* that it was not destroyed would blow him; he would be immediately shut down by Beijing, finished in Hong Kong, and no doubt could count his days.

Cold logic pointed to only one solution. Trained, conditioned through years of disciplined reaction, he was well aware of what was really required. But Tan, even before arriving at Fenton's apartment, knew that he wasn't going to follow through.

The film had been delivered to the only Chinese regime in which he believed. It was – as presented to him – a massive intelligence coup for Taipeh, however it might be exploited. Sammy Lin – 'Uncle Lam', introduced to Gerry Tan decades earlier at Cambridge – had been ecstatic at their last meeting. This 'mission accomplished' earned an accolade from the KMT's

Intelligence chief in Hong Kong. That was one thing. But for Gerry personally, the likely consequence now was that he would have to leave, go to ground in Taiwan – or even in the UK – and Peeble Hunt would find another Financial Director.

At the door, he stood and faced the man who was bringing an end to his extraordinary undercover vocation. He tensed, with a last nudge of indecision. Then he nodded, and unlatched the door himself.

'About Mrs Waley ...' he half turned as he went out. 'It was most regrettable, but there was no choice, you understand?'

'That's what I'm being paid for, isn't it – to understand? Fenton couldn't control it. It came out bitter and aggressive. The Chinese stared at him for an instant.

'Remember what they say about the gift horse,' said Gerry Tan softly. Then he was gone.

epilogue

GERRY TAN took early retirement from Peeble Hunt for 'personal and health reasons'. He invoked the same grounds for stopping his intelligence work for Beijing – to the great surprise and chagrin of his masters on the mainland. For the latter, Tan's exceptional last action was anyway a brilliant success: he had recovered and destroyed the secret material that the 'traitor' General Lin had taken out from The People's Republic of China.

Regret at Gerry Tan's retirement was naturally also shared by 'Uncle Lam', the KMT's intelligence chief in Hong Kong to whom Gerry had been reporting for years. The Nationalist regime on Taiwan, in which Gerry genuinely believed, was losing an invaluable asset.

Gerry Tan's sudden drop to 'low-profile' was in preparation for a permanent move to safety at short notice. The moment that Larry Fenton published his eyewitness story doubting the destruction of the film, fatal suspicion would fall on Tan, and Beijing would react decisively. After a few months of tense and inconclusive waiting, Gerry Tan went ahead and relocated. With Uncle Lam's administrative help, of course, Gerry and his family went to Taiwan. Only a few years later, they moved again – permanently, and further out of harm's way – to England. There, Gerry bought a house in the comfortable commuter belt at Gerrards Cross in Buckinghamshire.

As time went by, nothing relevant to the affair came out of Taiwan, nor did a Far East war scenario emerge – about which Colonel James Ma had warned the Americans. Not even a hint of the so-called 'Indictment' concerning Mao has appeared in the press anywhere. One might reasonably conclude, therefore, that caution prevailed in Taiwan – perhaps through dissension in the Military Command or lack of support from elsewhere.

Also, of course, contrary to Tan's fears, no newspaper, to this day, has published an 'I-was-there' account of Larry Fenton's momentous Hong Kong holiday.

Fenton packed up in Italy during the summer of 1978 and returned to settle in his Dorset cottage. Retired, except for writing occasional nature articles, he spends his time keeping the countryside from overrunning the garden and looking after Joanna who still commutes between Chudmore and London. The mass of notes on his week of a lifetime is stowed away in a drawer for use, so Larry Fenton says, in perhaps 'writing a bit of fiction sometime'.

*

Lou Appleton, the CIA officer in London to whom Colonel James Ma confided, *in extremis*, his war scenario fears, died a few years ago, aged 82. But early in his retirement, Appleton revisited London and stayed with an old MI6 colleague. After dinner one evening, he told the latter of his doubts, shared by a few other senior Agency officials, about the origins of the whole Indictment affair. For the MI6 friend, also retired, it was an anecdote worth remembering.

Based on information of various reliability, CIA analysts had pieced together an overall explanation, which was necessarily unsubstantiated, but, in the end, favoured. It concerned the very nature of the famous document itself.

This theory has it that the defection of General Lin was certainly genuine and caused a crisis reaction in Beijing, not least because of the vital military or other state secrets he would have taken with him. Emergency